WHERE'S THE *Groom?*

CATHRYN BROWN

Where's the Groom? is what authors call a "book of the heart." It's a book I love and am excited to share with you. But it doesn't fit the rules. It's half romance and half cozy mystery —with no dead body. It's also fun, so it has a dash of rom-com for good measure.

I wrote this at a time when I was watching a lot of movies from the 1930s and 1940s. Screwball comedies were popular then. They make you laugh and maybe groan occasionally at the humor. But you're smiling when it ends.

I hope you enjoy Summer and Cameron's story as much as I do!

CHAPTER ONE

"Woof! Woof!" a dog barked in a nearby yard.

Summer jumped and put her hand on her racing heart. "It's probably a pack of wild dogs that will attack any second. Thank you, Don Daily. I wouldn't be here if it wasn't for you, my wonderful groom," she muttered as she continued down the dark Nashville, Tennessee, sidewalk.

She'd wanted to call off her wedding for weeks, but every time she'd tried to pick up the phone or even tell him in person, she'd chickened out. Today, time had run out. She either had to tell him it was off or walk down the aisle, and, chicken that she was, she had put on the dress.

Only it seemed like he had found something more important to do.

Her brow furrowed. This address and Don's name had been on a large bouquet of white roses that had arrived at the church. She'd hoped Don had bought them, and for a reason that would give her a hint as to his whereabouts. But it simply didn't make sense that he'd abandoned her at one church, then gone to another. She shrugged. It wasn't much of a clue, but right now, it was her only clue.

Lifting the voluminous skirt of her wedding dress to the side, she carefully walked toward her destination. Both Don and his luggage were missing from his quarters at the inn he owned. As soon as she found him and told him their relationship was over, that it wasn't a reflection on him but completely about her, she could move on.

He had been her focus as she'd left the church on the other side of town, so she'd forgotten about the dress. Stumbling along the dark sidewalk, she really wished she'd remembered to change out of these high-heeled satin pumps.

Summer leaned against one of the big, old trees that lined the road, slipped off a shoe, and rubbed the arch of her foot. These shoes were barely comfortable enough to walk down the aisle in and certainly not built for a two-block trek down a sidewalk at night. She'd driven by the address and, after seeing it was a church, parked a couple of blocks away. She wanted to sneak up on it to see what was going on here. A woman in a wedding dress could be conspicuous.

After slipping the shoe back on, she walked toward the side of the building. Stepping onto the soft lawn, her feet felt instantly better. She'd been relieved that the clue had led her to a church; she wouldn't have wanted to visit an abandoned warehouse at ten o'clock at night.

Carefully looking around as she went, Summer made sure no one else was nearby. Nothing stirred. Not even a mouse. She stifled a giggle at the thought. Wow, she must be getting punchy.

The sound of voices drifted around from the front of the church. Slowly, ever so slowly, she peered around the corner of the building to look at the front door. The church's entrance glowed with light so bright that she blinked her eyes. When she could focus, she jumped back. A sobbing woman stood in front of the church, and a man was obviously comforting her.

Summer peered around the corner again, sighing in frustration when she got a clearer look. The man wore a white tuxedo and the woman a Hawaiian-print dress. They looked ordinary.

Who was she kidding? There wasn't anything normal about a man in a tuxedo and a sobbing woman in a Hawaiian-print dress standing outside a church late at night. But they didn't look like criminals.

She eyed the woman suspiciously. Maybe things were not as they appeared to be. Maybe the man and woman had kidnapped Don, and the woman regretted it. Maybe they were waiting here to meet a contact. Streetlights illuminated a limousine as it turned the corner a block away. When Summer pressed into the shadows to hide, the lace fabric of her dress caught on the brick building.

After gently pulling it away, she gathered the dress tightly against herself and peered around the corner.

Her eyes opened wide as the vehicle swung into the church parking lot. This was it! A long, black limousine pulled up to the front of the church. Then an older woman walked out of the church, put her arm around the younger, sobbing woman and helped her into the limo before climbing in beside her. The man closed the door, and the limo drove away with the two women.

And so did her clue. If they were just people in a church, the address on the flowers must have been a mistake from the flower shop. And if Don had nothing to do with the flowers, he had abandoned her at the altar. She may not have wanted to marry him, but to be left at the altar?

A tear slipped down one cheek, followed by another. Angrily swiping at her wet cheeks, Summer stepped away from the building in the direction of her car. Then she ran into a tree.

"Hey, there wasn't a tree—"

Very human hands touched her arms. Before she could scream, a hand clamped over her mouth. When she pushed with all of her weight against her captor, she was pulled closer to what was obviously a male body. Kicking at his shins, her right shoe flew away.

"Ouch." He flinched when her still-shod left foot made contact with his shin. "Don't move. I don't want to hurt you."

It's a man, and he doesn't want to hurt me. Isn't that what the criminal says just before he does something drastic? She shoved her body against his again, but he didn't budge.

"Please," he whispered, "I don't want to disturb the people in the church."

His sentence broke through her panic. *He doesn't want to disturb people in a church? Isn't it against the thug's code to care about things like that?* She stilled her body, but her breath came in ragged gasps under the pressure of his hand.

"Thank you." He released what was obviously a sigh of relief and fractionally relaxed his hold. "I want to know what you're doing here."

Great. The big oaf has obviously forgotten he has a hand clamped over my mouth. She nipped at his hand with her teeth.

"Sorry." He released her but didn't step away.

Squinting in the near total darkness, she tried to get a glimpse of his features. With only a vague outline visible, she gave up and stepped back. After brushing herself off and straightening her dress, she said, "Mr.?"

"Powers," he filled in.

She crossed her arms over her chest. "Mr. Powers, my heart is still racing from your assault. And you bruised my arms. Who do you think you are?"

"Miss? Mrs.? Ms.?"

She stood silently.

"Fine." He sounded annoyed. "I think I'm a man who saw a woman in a wedding dress skulking down the street, darting behind trees and hiding in the shadows of the church where my sister was supposed to be married. That's who I think I am."

Embarrassment replaced her anger and heat flooded her skin. At least it was dark enough that he couldn't see her blush. She searched her mind for a plausible excuse and decided on the whole truth. "I was supposed to get married today too."

"If I believe you, you have a reason for the dress. But not for sneaking around. Tell me why I shouldn't call the police."

She glared at him. Then she remembered he couldn't see her. "I can explain. As I was saying, I was supposed to get married today, but my fiancé Don Daily took off, and I'm looking for him."

"Don Daily?"

She nodded. "Do you know him?" Maybe this was the break she was searching for.

He leaned closer. "Don Daily?" he repeated. "Blond, about this tall"—he held a hand up to his eye level—"about twenty-eight?"

"Yes! You do know him. Do you know why he missed our wedding this afternoon?"

He looked heavenward and seemed to mutter a few words of prayer before looking at her again. "I wish I knew what was going on. He missed his wedding to my sister tonight."

Summer laughed, but it sounded strained even to her ears. "That can't be my Don. My Don missed our wedding."

The man shook his head. "Come inside." He reached for her arm. She wanted to push him away, but she needed answers, so, wobbling on one shoe, she walked beside him into the church.

Inside, he gently pushed her into the back pew. "Wait here. I'll be right back."

Staring into space, she thought about what he'd said. Don? Marrying another woman? Had he planned to be a bigamist? She shook her head. There were obviously two very similar men with the same name. Unlikely, yes, but not impossible.

The man came back and handed her a cup of water. She squinted in the dim light of the church but still couldn't clearly see his face.

"Here, drink this."

Summer stood and held out the cup of water to him. "This is all a mistake. We can't be talking about the same man."

"Does your Don Daily own 1902 Inn?"

Summer nodded. "See, it can't be . . ." She stopped talking and looked up at him. When he nodded, she tried to take a sip of the water, but instead the cup slipped slowly out of her hand and hit the ground. Blinking, she tried to look up at him as the lights dimmed and swirled around her.

It seemed like seconds later that she was staring up at two women she didn't know. One was chafing her wrist, the other patting her cheek. They appeared to be sweet old ladies about her grandmother's age. Struggling to get up, she wondered what held her back. Then she looked down and saw the yards of fabric of a wedding dress twisted around her body.

Was this some sort of dream?

A handsome man with dark brown hair stepped into her line of sight.

Yep, it was a dream.

"Are you all right?"

As soon as he spoke, it all came back to her. Don had left her *and* the man's sister at the altar.

CHAPTER TWO

Summer stretched and yawned. Then she burrowed further under the covers. Something about today didn't seem right, but she couldn't put her finger on it. Then she remembered. Sitting upright, she swung her legs over the edge of the bed.

She should be married to Don Daily. She should be on a honeymoon. Sure, she'd decided to call it off, but for months she'd pictured this day. Don had kept the destination a secret, but she'd hoped for something warm and balmy, somewhere they could get away from everyone and enjoy each other. His only clue for her was that the location had a climate similar to Middle Tennessee. It wasn't exactly tropical here in October. Spain might be similar. Or maybe he'd booked a Greek island cruise.

Right now, she had a bigger question—where was Don?

Glancing around her bedroom, she relaxed. She'd decorated the room in different shades of blue and loved the soothing effect. Something white in the corner of the room caught her attention. Her wedding dress lay draped over a chair. A single white shoe sat on the floor under it.

Summer bounced onto the carpet, then plunked back down on the bed. "Ouch." Rubbing her feet, she remembered her late-night walk to the church. She pulled her robe off the end of the bed, put it on, and gently padded over to the kitchen. She could see herself walking to the church, but . . .

She froze. How had she gotten home? Last night, she'd watched while two women had stepped into a limo and had driven off. She had stood outside the church in the dark and run into Don's other bride's brother.

Pacing around the floor, she ignored her sore feet. What had happened after that? She knew that after she'd fainted, she'd looked up at two older ladies and a very handsome man. If she'd driven home, she should have some memory of the drive. Studying her condominium's parking lot from her living room window, she searched for her silver car. It wasn't there.

How had she gotten home? Filling the kettle with water for tea, she tried to remember. When she set the kettle on the stove, something blue on her counter caught her eye: a page torn from the pad she had for her grocery list.

Miss Collier,

You were in no condition to drive, so I brought you home. Please call and either I or one of my family members will pick you up and take you back to your car.

Cameron Powers

(P.S. I asked my grandmother to look in your purse for your address and keys. She also tucked you into bed.)

. . .

Beneath his signature, he had included his phone number. Summer read the note three times. A man she'd just met had driven her here, and his grandmother had tucked her into bed. The noise from the whistling kettle barely got through her muddled mind.

Reaching for a mug and loose tea leaves, she prepared her tea and thought about her wedding day. What had happened to simply walking down the aisle? It had sounded like such a good idea when Don had proposed months ago.

She pushed those thoughts aside and sat at her table with her hands huddled around the mug of Earl Grey. What she needed was a plan for today. A plan would bring a sense of order. She first needed to retrieve her car.

Today was Saturday, so no one would expect her to be in her office. Besides, she'd told all of her marketing consulting firm's clients that she was getting married and going on a week-long honeymoon, so they wouldn't expect her for a while.

Groaning, she leaned her head on the table. Now, she had the embarrassing task of telling everyone she hadn't gotten married. Maybe she could hide inside her condo today. And next week.

She'd enjoyed her home since she'd bought it a year ago. But she'd looked forward to living at the inn. It seemed so warm and comfortable. Nashville had been a lonely place until she'd started spending time there with Don.

Walking over to her closet, jeans and a sweater called to her. With the bottom half on and the top halfway over her head, the phone rang. She muttered, "It's probably someone wanting to know more about what happened yesterday." On the sixth ring, she decided to pick it up.

An Officer Smith introduced himself.

"Officer? From the military?"

"No, miss," he said, "from the police department. We wanted to check on you. Someone ransacked Don Daily's quarters and a guest room at the 1902 Inn. Do you know anything that can shed light on this situation?"

Summer gasped. "Nothing. Can I help?" Only yesterday morning, she'd expected to get married—unless she backed out—and have a normal, calm life. Now, Don was gone, and she was getting phone calls from law enforcement professionals.

"We'll let you know if we have any news or any further questions. For the time being, look carefully wherever you go. We don't know why someone did this, but we do know your fiancé is missing, and there may be a criminal element at work here."

Criminals? "Yes, officer."

After he ended the call, Summer stared at her phone. She'd just gone from being one of two fiancées to one of two fiancées with a groom who might need help. She walked across the room, turned, and came back. It didn't make any sense.

Summer took a deep breath and released it. She needed to clear her head, and a walk beside the lake always performed that miracle for her.

Thankfully, Centennial Park sat only a couple of blocks from her condo. Wearing her most comfortable sneakers, she wandered along the pond, the wind licking at her hair. The cloudy, windy day seemed to match her mood. Finally, feeling the bite of the wind, she sat on a bench and huddled into her jacket.

Scenes from last night and this morning kept playing in her mind. "Let the police department take care of everything," she repeated over and over again, hoping it would sink in.

Maybe Don had met with foul play, but she thought it more likely that it all had something to do with his two brides-to-be. She realized that the police might not know about the second bride. Cozy, the desk clerk at the inn, had probably given information about her, Bride #1, to them. But she didn't know about Bride #2.

Should she let them handle things or do whatever she could to help? For a brief time, she'd thought she loved Don.

The sun broke through the clouds, lifting her indecision along with the gloom. On the off chance that Don was in trouble, she'd do everything she could to help him, just as she would help a friend. As she walked back to her condo, she formulated a plan.

The police would have no idea if something was missing or new in Don's quarters, so a thorough search was in order. She'd spent enough time there in the last four months, working on paperwork for the inn and helping to entertain his guests, to be an expert.

First, she'd retrieve her car from the church. Once she had independence again, she'd quickly find Don. Her plan was foolproof.

By the time she sat in a taxi, it was early afternoon. Even though Cameron had offered to have someone from his family take her to her car, she knew that would be too embarrassing. As the car neared her destination, she watched out the window, and they parked in front of the church she'd only seen in the dark.

As she handed the driver her money, a man near the church unlocked the door on a newer blue pickup. Something about him and his movements seemed familiar. He had dark, wavy hair, and was tall and handsome. She stared for a moment, then turned away. Bride #2's brother. Cameron. She stepped out of the taxi and averted her head so Cameron couldn't see her face.

Just when she thought she'd made a clean break of it and wouldn't have to relive the humiliation of the night before, she heard, "Summer! Wait!" Turning slowly around, she pinned on a smile that she hoped looked happy.

He closed the door on his truck and hurried over. "You should have called."

She shrugged.

A few seconds later, he said, "I think I understand why you couldn't call. By the way, do you have any more information about Don?"

"The police don't know where he is."

He looked confused. "The police? He hasn't been missing long enough to be a missing person."

"When they discovered that his quarters at the inn had been ransacked, they decided there must be more going on than meets the eye."

He stared at her.

"Honestly. I couldn't make this up, could I?"

He smiled, and she felt it to her toes. Wow, could this man smile.

"My sister asked me to keep an eye on the situation."

"Where is she?"

"Mom thought it best for her to get away from here. The two of them left in the limo last night and used the Hawaiian honeymoon reservations. My sister had paid for the trip, so she decided she'd go."

"She did? Don paid for ours." *But to where?* she wondered again.

Cameron's lips were moving.

"Huh?"

"I said, why don't we go somewhere and talk about everything that's happened?"

He seemed sincere, but she didn't want him or any man around right now.

"Thank you, but I'll figure this out," she said in her most businesslike voice.

"Summer, my family is involved in this. I was almost related to Don Daily." He said Don's name in a disgusted way that told her he hadn't been happy about that situation.

Summer shook her head.

"I'm going to find out what happened to him," he said, then confirmed her earlier thoughts. "I might not have wanted Don to marry my sister, but he's run out on her, and she needs closure on this. I will find him so he can apologize to her in person when she returns." He paused before continuing. "It may be easier to work together to find him."

Summer looked up and sighed. He was right. He was absolutely right. "Okay, but I call the shots."

"We work together," he said with a finality to his voice.

"Together," she agreed grudgingly.

Glancing at his watch, he said, "I came over here to check on the church and make sure everything had been cleaned up. I have something planned with my family tonight. I know tomorrow's Sunday, but I need to finish up a project at my office. Can we meet later in the day after work?"

Summer stared at him, unable to think of a plausible reason why not.

"How about dinner?"

She started to protest.

He smiled. "You eat, don't you?"

Smiling against her will, she said, "Yes, I do eat. I even know of a wonderful little Italian restaurant over in Germantown. Mama Maria's Ristorante."

"Fine. I'll meet you there tomorrow at five-thirty." He glanced at his watch again and started for his truck. "See you there," he called over his shoulder.

Summer followed Cameron out of the neighborhood, parting when he went one way on the interstate and she went the other. He had been very nice but also quite insistent. If she'd had a brother, she'd have wanted one like him. She put on her turn signal to change lanes. She'd agreed to dinner, but what did she actually know about him?

He was Cameron Powers. No one would have staged a phony wedding to throw her off the scent. Or would they? She whipped into the right lane and pulled off at the next exit. Someone might if the stakes were high enough. How high were they? What was going on?

She pulled into a grocery store's parking lot and searched on her phone for anything about a Cameron Powers in the Nashville area. She found one. The address next to his name was out in Belle Meade, about twenty minutes from here. Was this him? Straightening her shoulders, she decided to take the time for a little detective work.

Leaving, she drove by the front of the grocery store and noticed a newspaper box. That got her thinking about newspapers. Many engagements were announced in them. Hers had been. What about this supposed second wedding? If it had been in one of the area's newspapers, people would have noticed and said something to her.

Pulling back onto the Interstate, she headed for Belle Meade and Mr. Cameron Powers. When she turned onto his street, the sky blazed with a fiery sunset. Sitting in her car, she studied the area. He lived in a graceful, older neighborhood with massive oak trees towering over houses and beautifully landscaped gardens filled with flowers.

After dark, she'd sneak up to the house and peer in a window to verify that the man she'd met as Cameron Powers matched the actual person. Other than sitting here all night hoping to catch him when he left in the morning, that seemed like the easiest way to check. It was only a bit creepy on her part. After what she'd been through, though, she had to protect herself.

As the sun set over the horizon, lights came on in many of the houses. It was time. Grateful she wore jeans and loafers, she casually walked up to his address. It was a brand-new house under construction, so an older one must have been torn down. Could it be the right home then? She didn't think a house under construction would have been listed online. Continuing past it, she turned to look back.

On the second story, lights were on at the back of the house, shining into what she saw of the backyard. She snuck around back to check it out. Light poured out of French doors that opened to a two-story vertical drop. There would obviously be a deck when the house was finished, but it wasn't there now. So much for looking in a window to see who lived here.

Going around front, she studied the house. Temporary-looking stairs went from the street to the unlit front entrance with a small landing at the top. The front half of the house was dark. Maybe if she peered through the front windows, she could see through to the lit back. Glancing around to make sure no neighbors watched from a window, she stealthily crept up the stairs, thankful as she reached the top that none had creaked.

On his front porch, a shadow moved across the side of the house. Someone must be moving around inside. She stepped backward into a shadowy corner.

"Rowr!" a cat yelled.

She jumped off a cat's tail and put her hand to her racing heart. Now an innocent cat had been caught in this situation. She heard footsteps coming toward the door. Hurrying down the stairs as quickly as possible without making noise, she reached the bottom and ducked out of sight just as the front door opened. She peered around the corner.

A man who wasn't Cameron Powers stepped outside. "Mildred, are you all right?"

A cat meowed.

Who would name their cat *Mildred*?

"Everything okay?" another male voice yelled from inside.

"She looks fine. Let's watch the game," the man yelled back.

The door closed, cutting off that method of looking inside. She couldn't sneak back onto the porch tonight because they'd come check out any sounds. What now? Before she trusted Cameron Powers, she had to know more.

There must be a way to see inside this house. She had the answer. *This beautiful old neighborhood has big trees behind all the houses.* She'd been a champion tree climber as a kid, so this would be easy. *If* she remembered how. Summer crouched and moved stealthily toward the trees. A large, old oak with low branches sat directly ahead. Reaching up to the branch, she swung onto it and smiled with satisfaction.

Positioned straight back from the windows with lights, this tree would allow her to see inside the house once she'd climbed high enough. Stretching for the next branch, she kept climbing, glancing toward the house at each new branch. Finally, she reached the right level.

Tucking her hair behind her ears, she watched three men who sat in front of a large screen TV—the man who'd checked on the cat, a man with red hair, and another man with dark-brown hair, like Cameron. But was it him? She leaned forward, hoping to see him more clearly.

"Meow."

Looking down, she could barely see a cat in the shadows under the tree. Probably Mildred.

The meowing got louder and more insistent. Almost like an alarm. Suddenly, a back light came on, and Cameron stood at the window, looking right at her.

She had to get out of here.

CHAPTER THREE

*D*ropping from branch to branch, she slipped to the ground and came face to face with Cameron Powers.

"Who is it?" asked the man who'd come to the front door to check on the cat.

Cameron turned her into the light. "Summer Collier, I'd like you to meet my younger brothers, Luke"—he pointed at the redhead—"and John."

Summer nodded.

"So you're the one who tried to take our sister's fiancée," John said angrily.

"No!"

"John." Cameron said, putting his hand on his brother's shoulder. "She's the one who was left at the altar just like our sister."

John acquiesced to his older brother's words and didn't say any more. But he silently glared at her.

Summer's mind was in a whirlwind. Had she stolen Don

from an innocent woman and later discovered she didn't even want to marry him? "When did your sister become engaged?"

Cameron interrupted. "Let's go inside."

Summer walked beside them. When they got to the lighted front steps, she noticed Mildred was beside her. The cat seemed to be looking at her with a "thought you could sneak in here, huh?" expression. Summer shook her head.

Once inside, John continued to glare at her, but Luke seemed friendly. He actually smiled and answered her question about the engagement. "I remember the date of the engagement. July tenth, Mom's birthday."

Summer sighed with relief. She hadn't wanted to play the role of usurper. "I've been engaged since the first week of June," she said as she glanced around.

This was the room she'd seen from the tree, and it included a large living room, kitchen, and dining room. The inside of the house appeared almost complete. The plywood-clad kitchen floor needed to be covered, and some trim around the windows needed to be finished, but, even in its incomplete state, she could tell it would be a beautiful home. High ceilings over large rooms. Wood floors in the living room. Gorgeous dark-wood cabinets in the kitchen. Just her taste.

"I don't want to seem rude, but why were you in my tree, Summer?"

Blushing, she stared at the floor. "I wanted to make sure that you really were Cameron Powers, not a criminal pretending to be Cameron Powers. I looked up your address online, and here I am." She studied the trim molding on the wall.

He started laughing.

Summer turned toward him.

Laughing harder, he held onto his midsection and leaned against the wall next to the couch. Just when she thought he'd fall, the laughter slowed. Grinning, he sat on the couch and wiped tears from his eyes. "Summer, you really are something."

His brothers stared at him as if he'd lost his mind.

"Boys, you've got to remember that this woman came to the church late last night in a wedding dress, and now we find her up my tree. She's unstoppable. I'd like to have her on my side."

Startled, Summer grinned. Even John looked a little softer now. She moved toward the door. "I'll see you tomorrow then." As Luke opened it for her, she turned back. "By the way, how can you be building a house and already be listed online at this address?"

"I tore down a small older house to build mine. I lived in it for a year while I worked on the plans for my dream house."

"You designed this?" Summer gestured to the room.

Luke answered, "Cameron is the finest architect in the South."

Cameron said, "Spoken like a loyal sibling."

She would have loved to have a home like this. "It's beautiful."

"Thank you." As she started to walk out the door, he added, "Wait. I have something that belongs to you. I found it when I brought my grandmother back to her car last night." He disappeared down a hallway and returned with her missing wedding shoe. "I thought about having it delivered by an actor wearing a powdered wig and a royal-looking costume."

A man in costume walking into her office presented such a startling image that Summer laughed. "I didn't think I could laugh about this so soon." She took the shoe and tucked it under her arm. "I'll see you tomorrow. You'll like Mama Maria's."

When she left, all three men were smiling. Even the cat seemed to be coming over to her side. Mildred sat quietly by the door when she walked through it.

Cameron remained on her mind as she drove toward the inn. She had almost a day until their scheduled dinner and might be able to solve the whole mystery before then. Had she done the right thing in agreeing to work with him?

Yes. Besides, he'd been quite insistent. He would be there whether she let him work with her or not. And he might be helpful. From somewhere deep inside, she heard, *He's very nice and handsome too.* She dismissed that thought and tried to focus on the mysterious whereabouts of her groom.

Thinking about Don made her wonder about Cameron's sister, Bride #2. Why had Don proposed to another woman when he'd already been engaged? Had he seen something in his second fiancée that she didn't have?

As she pulled off at her exit, she realized that she shouldn't try to put herself in Don's mind. She'd help him by solving the mystery, and she hoped he hadn't come to any harm. But that was it.

At the inn, she decided to go through the back door to Don's quarters. The path curving to the rear of the inn had lights lining it at night, and she could avoid all the guests in the lobby. Walking around the peaceful building almost erased yesterday and all that had happened since.

She could hear traffic in the distance but always felt as though she'd stepped back in time at the historic building.

As Summer turned the corner, someone coming from the other direction ran into her. "Oomph." She fell backward against the hedge that lined the path. Pushing her long hair off her face, she saw Cozy lying against the other side's hedge.

"Summer, I'm so glad to see you. I saw your car pull in and hoped to catch you here. Do you know what's happened at the inn?"

Summer stood and brushed herself off. "The police called earlier."

Cozy pushed against the hedge and stood. "Mr. Daily's quarters are a mess. Someone ripped them apart. Room 214 is the same way." Both her blonde-and-blue curls and her outrageous red dangle earrings bobbed while she spoke. "He's been kidnapped!" Usually overdramatizing things, Cozy probably had now.

"I'm sure they'll find him."

Cozy nodded vigorously. Summer smiled as the earrings nodded too.

Then the other woman went in the back door of the inn and back to her job at the front desk.

At the door to Don's quarters, Summer found yellow police tape blocking the entry. She stood on the walk, tapping her foot. Should she take off the tape? In the movies, removing the tape was always against the law.

She walked over to the inn's back door and entered the lobby. Summer couldn't help admiring the hardwood floors, high ceilings, and curved, wide stairway. She'd always found the inn inviting and beautiful.

From where she stood, she could also see yellow tape

across the lobby entrance to Don's quarters. *That can't have helped business.* "Cozy, there's police tape on Don's door."

Cozy thumped her forehead with the palm of her hand. "I'm amazed that I forgot to mention that earlier. Guests commented on it as they checked out."

"I want to go through his place and see if I can tell if anything is missing."

"They won't let you. They said"—she stopped for a second, then deepened her voice—"'This is a crime scene. No one is to enter.'"

Summer grinned in spite of herself. As a child, Cozy's little sister couldn't say "Camille," her real name, but instead had called her "Cozy." The nickname had stuck. Cozy had told her she enjoyed the simpler name. A college student with slightly unconventional clothing and hair, she'd won Summer over with her charm during the interview. Summer had urged Don to hire her over the "more suitable" applicants for his generally staid and conventional inn and, unusually for him, he had.

"Maybe the police will let me go in if I ask. Hand me the phone."

Ten very frustrating minutes later, Summer had permission to enter but not to disturb anything.

"Phew." She set the phone down and purposefully strode over to the door. Cozy followed behind her as she stepped under the tape and entered the room.

Don's employee hadn't overdramatized this. Walking around the large room that contained his living and sleeping quarters, Summer stopped to smooth her hand over what had been a beautiful wingback chair. Upholstery, pillows, and even the mattress on his bed had been slit and the stuffing pulled out. Pictures were out of their frames.

Someone had opened every desk and dresser drawer, strewing the contents around the room. One painting still in its frame lay on the floor. Picking it up, she looked around for a place to put it, settling on the wingback chair.

"I hope all this"—Summer waved her hand to encompass the room—"hasn't disturbed the guests too much."

"Almost all the guests have left. The only one that's still here is in room 205. Mr. Breznowski. You know, the man with the Eastern European accent who comes here every couple of months."

"Oh, yes. He just sits in his room for a day or two, then leaves."

Cozy shivered. "It's kind of spooky."

Summer laughed. "Maybe he has business here or something. Does he get phone calls?"

"Yes." Cozy visibly relaxed. "I'm sure you're right." She looked around the room. "What a mess."

Summer agreed. "This is a mess."

"Our housekeeper, Emilie, isn't going to be happy when she has to straighten this up."

"I wonder if they were looking for something," Summer said thoughtfully. First, she'd check his appointment book and see if he'd had anything scheduled that might give a clue.

But where was it? Nothing was where it should be. She could start on one side of the room with Cozy on the other. And while they worked, she'd ask Cozy if she knew about Bride #2.

"Cozy—" The phone ringing in the lobby interrupted her, and Cozy ran to answer it. The girl had enough to do.

The time had almost reached midnight when Summer finished her search. No book.

After another frustrating call to the police department,

Summer decided to quit for the night. With all this mess, a missing appointment book didn't interest them. She knew better, though. Don wrote down everything he planned to do. It could be important.

Back at her condo, she went straight to bed. Exhausted physically, her busy mind continued to whirr. The wedding that didn't happen. Cameron. The mess at the inn. As she lay in bed, a plan of action formed in her mind. Tomorrow morning she would . . .

She paused her planning. Her week had been so crazy that she'd lost track of time. Her wedding should have been two days ago. Today had been . . . Saturday.

She'd go to church tomorrow morning. Then she'd do some more research. She would find out everything she could about Mr. Cameron Powers and his reputation as an architect. What had brought his sister into Don's life, and why was he demanding to help search for Don?

She rolled onto her side. She'd also do a little research on her missing fiancé. Maybe his mother or a business associate could shed light on the situation. Yes, she thought as she fell asleep, first Cameron, then Don. No. She fought to stay awake. Don came first. Then Cameron.

On her way home from church the next morning, she thought about being married. She'd wanted a man to spend time with and a place that felt like home. Both Don and the inn had fit those requirements.

That dream had turned into a nightmare.

She needed to dream bigger, because she was still picking up the pieces from the last dream. She had to elevate her expectations. After thinking for a minute, she decided she wanted a man filled with joy and laughter, a man who would cherish her and spend a lifetime with her. Cameron's face came to mind, but she pushed it out of the way. He was simply an assistant in this mystery. Her Dr. Watson.

CHAPTER FOUR

*D*ialing her *almost* mother-in-law's phone number, Summer thought about how to approach her. Considering recent events, she probably should have called her sooner.

Thinking about Don's mother brought little emotion. Everyone else seemed to talk about their mother-in-law fondly or not-so-fondly. But Summer had never spoken to her and only knew her first name because she was on her son's list of wedding guests and had required an invitation.

At the last minute, though, Don had told his mother not to come to the wedding. He'd said she didn't need to make the long trip from Florida. That he and his new wife would visit her. *Sure, he'd planned to visit her, but with which woman in the role of wife?*

She'd have to tread lightly. Mrs. Daily might not know about anything that had happened here recently.

When a woman answered the phone, Summer tried for an easy tone, "Mrs. Daily, this is Don's fiancée."

"Erin?"

"No . . ." she said slowly. That must be his other fiancée's name. "This is Summer."

"Oh hi, dear. Don said he wasn't sure about choosing between you and Erin."

I can do this, Summer thought. *I can help Don. Even if he told his mother about having two fiancées and that doesn't seem to bother her.*

"What can I do for you?"

Focus, Summer. Focus. "I haven't seen Don for a couple of days and wondered if you'd heard from him."

"No, dear. A nice officer from the police department asked me the same thing."

"Did you mention Erin to him?"

"I'm not sure that I did. Do you think he's with her?"

By this point, she could tell that his mother didn't have any useful information. "No, Mrs. Daily. I know where Erin is. You have a great day."

"You too, dear. Tell Don to call me."

Summer hung up the phone and almost laughed. Almost. Even his mother had known about the two women. How had he approached that conversation? *Mother, I'm getting married. I'll tell you my wife's name that day.*

Even though it was Sunday, she called a couple of clients she knew well, hoping they might have information she didn't know about Don or Cameron. Nothing. Picking up the phone, she decided to try one more. She'd worked on a special marketing project for this woman a few months ago.

As expected, Don's behavior baffled her. But when Summer asked about an architect named Cameron Powers, the woman laughed. "My dear, that man is the most talented architect I've seen in years. He designed a house for some friends and they are thrilled."

"So he's one of the better architects working in Nashville?"

She laughed again. "He's working far beyond this area. There are houses he's designed everywhere from Alaska to Florida. Beautiful, large houses."

Summer thought for a moment. Should she risk asking about his character?

"Why the questions?" the woman asked.

Summer hesitated before answering. Then she thought of the perfect way to word it. "His family knew Don, so he's been interested in Don's whereabouts. I wanted to be sure of his trustworthiness."

"You can rest assured that this man's reputation is spotless. He's known as an honest businessman. And he's quite handsome. Don't you agree?"

Wrapped up in her thoughts, Summer didn't think before speaking. "Yes, he's gorgeous." The woman's laughter made her realize what she'd said. "I mean—"

"Someone's just arriving." Summer could hear voices and laughter in the background. "By the way, I'll have a new project for you soon. I'll call or stop by your office when I know more."

The phone hung up in her ear. Setting it down, Summer knew she had no reason to leave Cameron out of the search. And there was a bonus. Grinning, she thought, *He is gorgeous.*

Of course, she'd decide how to proceed with Don's disappearance. No matter what Cameron Powers thought, he was working with her. She wasn't working with him. She'd make that clear at dinner tonight.

～

Coming from opposite directions of the parking lot, she and Cameron approached the door of Mama Maria's. She'd traded her jeans for black pants because she'd assumed he would come directly from his office and would be more formally dressed. He arrived in a businesslike, light-green sweater and tan pants. He looked gorgeous, as usual. He also looked serious.

"My sister called this afternoon wanting to know about Don. When I told her he hadn't been found, she burst into tears." He continued talking as they walked inside. "Though I hadn't ever been thrilled about her choice of husband and am quite relieved that the wedding is off, I still couldn't upset her more by telling her about you."

She'd been right about his feelings toward Don. Summer spoke quietly. "She has to know. Knowing about Don's other fiancée might make it easier to forget him."

Once seated, Cameron stayed with the subject. "Did it make it easier for you?"

She picked up her menu. "Let's order."

"Summer, it might help Erin if I understand."

She looked over the top of the menu. "Finding him will help. Talking to him will help. Knowing about his second fiancée . . ." She shrugged. "But I think it's better than not knowing. And better than crying."

"I'll tell her tomorrow. And together, you and I will find him."

Summer felt a burst of happiness. This man that she barely knew wanted to help her. Don wouldn't have done that much to find Cameron unless he had been lost in the inn. What had she been doing with a man who liked having her around but didn't truly seem to want her in his life?

When Cameron picked up his menu, the waiter walked

over to the table to explain the specials. Cameron took her recommendation of lasagna and, as soon as the waiter walked away, asked, "Now, start at the beginning. Tell me everything that happened. And please include how you found the church."

When she finished, he leaned back in his seat. "I know my sister was engaged to Don Daily. I read your engagement announcement in the newspaper, so I know you were also engaged to him. All of this would sound impossible otherwise."

"You checked up on me?" She felt her hackles rise. This man hadn't taken her at her word?

He raised an eyebrow. "You're a professional, intelligent woman, and you climbed my tree to check me out. I went a simpler route and read the newspaper article online."

"You may have a point." His words sank in. "You also said I was a professional, intelligent woman."

"After the tree event, I did some research. You own Creativity, a marketing firm with an excellent reputation."

Pride rushed through her. She'd spent the last two years working to establish her business.

"Did you do work for Don's inn?"

"Yes, that's how we met." Their conversation brought her thoughts back to the church where she'd run into Cameron. "By the way, what happened after you told me about Don? There were two older ladies leaning over me . . ."

"My grandmother and her sister. You fainted after I told you about my sister. When you came to, you just laid there and repeated over and over that you were going 'to find that jerk and wring his neck.'"

She covered her face with her hands. "No. I couldn't have."

"You did, but don't worry, those women and I were about the only people still at the church. While they stayed with you and searched through your purse for information, I brought my car to the front of the church. Then I picked you up, carried you to my car, and my grandmother and I drove you home."

She felt humiliated to her bones. "Thank you," she whispered.

"Summer, I was happy to be able to help. I hope that my sister would have someone take care of her if I couldn't."

After the waiter brought their salads, Summer slowly picked up her fork and thought about the mystery. How should they approach it?

Cameron interrupted her thoughts. "I haven't seen or heard of anyone mentioning the two-fiancée story on social media or the news. Have you?"

"Thankfully, nothing. Just a story last night on one station about Don's quarters and a guest room being ransacked." She leaned forward. "Almost as a footnote, they mentioned a fiancée abandoned at the altar, but they didn't even have a photo of me. And I don't think the police know about Bride #2."

"Bride #2?"

"Your sister."

"Erin."

"That's what Don's mother said."

Cameron blew out a deep breath. "She knew? This is strange." He rested his elbows on the table and tapped his fingers on his chin. "I wonder if we should tell the police about Erin."

"Don is missing and his quarters have been ransacked. Would she know any more about that than I do? And if the story about her gets in the papers, it may expose her to public ridicule."

Cameron took another bite of his salad. "I keep picturing my sobbing sister." A moment later, he whispered, "Not telling feels like I'm withholding evidence."

Summer studied a piece of tomato as she pushed it around her salad bowl with her fork. Looking up, she said, "Let's wait a day."

"One day." He thought about it. "That should be fine."

"By the way, why didn't the newspaper print her engagement announcement?"

"I asked my mother about that once. Don wanted to keep their wedding personal, he said, just between them and the family. Of course, we both now know why he didn't want it in the newspapers."

"Yes." She laid her fork down.

"Are you sure you want to search for him?"

"I had planned to marry him. I owe him this much."

Cameron eyed their lasagna hungrily when the waiter brought it over. Taking a bite, he sighed. "This is great."

"I wouldn't steer you wrong. You know, I'm surprised Don's appointment book is missing. The person who ransacked the inn must have stolen it."

He paused with a bite of lasagna halfway to his mouth. "Tell me why you think the appointment book is important."

"Don wrote everything down and paid a great deal of attention to his appointment book. He had his life neatly organized."

"It took amazing organizational skills to be engaged to two women," he muttered.

Summer didn't reply to his comment. The unfortunate thing was that he was right. Returning to her earlier thoughts, she said, "Anything that used to be in his quarters and isn't there now should be important."

"That's something I can agree with you about. Let's go look over his quarters after dinner."

"Tonight?"

"We both work during the day, so we'll have to do our sleuthing after work and on the weekends."

As she drove to the inn, Summer wished she could work on the mystery on her own and send Cameron on his way. Dinner had been fine, and he seemed like a nice guy, but this whole situation with Don had stressed her out. Cameron added one more thing to the mix. Sighing, she realized it might be helpful if two people searched.

When they entered the lobby, Cozy studied Cameron from head to toe. Then she looked over at Summer with a question in her eyes. Who was this handsome man?

How could she explain Cameron? "Cozy, this is Cameron. He's going to help me search Don's quarters. He's—" She looked at Cameron for help.

"A friend," he supplied.

She smiled gratefully at him. "Yes, a friend."

Cozy looked from one of them to the other. "No one's been in Mr. Daily's quarters since you were here last night."

Summer opened the door to her former fiancé's private rooms that were separate from his office and ducked under the yellow tape. "The housekeeper certainly hasn't been here."

Cameron followed her. Walking around the room, he said, "Someone wanted something."

"I know." Standing in front of Don's desk, she pointed at the couch. "Why don't you begin over there and I'll start here?"

Opening the desk drawer, she let out a strangled cry. "How—" The appointment book lay exactly where it should. "It was missing. No one will help me if they don't believe me." She leaned against the desk.

Cameron hurried over. "I believe you."

"You do?"

He nodded. Then he picked up the book with a confused expression on his face.

She walked over to Don's small couch and stared at the pile of debris that littered it. She thought about shoving the mess onto the floor but decided against it. The police had said to leave everything as she'd found it. "Let's go out to the lobby and go through his calendar on the couch."

When they arrived there, Cameron asked about getting her a cup of tea.

Summer smiled at him. "How'd you know I love tea?"

"When I wrote the note at your kitchen counter, I felt like I'd stumbled into a tea shop. You had a large basket with boxes and tins of tea, shelves with assorted cups and mugs, plus a little basket with a collection of the things you put loose tea in."

"Tea balls and strainers. Yes, I'd love a cup of green tea. Ask at the inn's restaurant. They'll make mine and whatever you want too."

He came back a few minutes later with her tea and a mug of coffee for himself. "Now, let's see what's important enough to steal."

After an hour, Summer threw the book down and rubbed her tired eyes. "We went through this from January first to December thirty-first and still have no clues. Or even an idea of what to do now. The only thing we know for sure is that he missed an appointment to meet with his printer about some brochures. Oh yes, and he's planning to have a Christmas party on December twelfth."

"He did lead a boring life."

Summer glared at him. "He's an innkeeper. His business kept him busy."

"Didn't he ever take you out?"

"Of course we went out. We've gone to . . ." She looked out the window and thought. "I know we've gone out. Give me a minute." Stunned, she looked at him. She wouldn't admit it, but she couldn't think of anywhere they had gone together, other than the inn or her office. "I know he must have, but I can't think of a time."

"And why weren't the weddings in the appointment book?"

"No man can forget his own wedding."

Cameron shrugged and looked over at her. He got grouchy whenever she mentioned Don. Of course, Don had hurt his sister. "You're right about knowing when you're supposed to get married. He kept track of two weddings."

Summer winced.

"I'm sorry, Summer." He put his hand on her shoulder. "You were wounded by him too." He even apologized nicely. "It's getting late. Why don't we look around Don's quarters one more time? If we don't find anything, we head home."

Summer watched Cameron stand. She had come to think of the inn as home, but the way Cameron said the word made her think of rose gardens and picket fences. It had such a warm, secure sound. Passing through Don's living area, she picked up the painting she had put on the wingback chair. It had an expensive look to it, but she knew it had to be an inexpensive print. At least one item in the room remained undamaged.

When she was setting the painting back on the chair, Cameron tripped over something and caught himself on the table next to her. The painting missed the chair and, as she watched, cringing, it flipped and fell facedown, intact, on the floor. Something white was wedged into the frame.

"Look! Look!" She knelt on the floor in front of the painting, and Cameron crouched beside her.

"There's a piece of paper stuck in here." As she reached for it, he grabbed her hand. Warmth tingled through her fingertips, up her arm and all the way down to her toes.

She leaned backward, sliding her hand away from his, then stared at him dumbfounded. What was it about this man? He was nice *and* made her tingle?

"Summer?" He waved his hand in front of her face.

She looked into his chocolate-brown eyes. "What?"

"Don't touch the paper. It might have fingerprints. We should call the police now and let them take care of it."

She felt like a fool. How could she have gotten pulled in by a touch and a pair of brown eyes? She'd solve this mystery.

She'd look into his eyes later.

ocus, Summer. Focus. Staring at the paper in the frame, she felt her head clear. "I want to read it first. Maybe I'll understand what it says and solve this mystery." *And get back to life as usual,* she added to herself.

Cameron started sputtering protest.

"Wait, I'll be right back." She raced out of the room. The inn's kitchen had exactly what they needed.

When she walked back in, she found Cameron crouched beside the frame, rocking it back and forth. He pushed it one way and put his face right up to the note, then rocked it the other way and did it again. Summer stood there and watched him. What was he doing?

After she asked that very question, he looked up sheepishly. "When I moved the frame, the folded paper opened, so I thought I'd try moving it back and forth. I could read a couple of letters—A and K—without touching it."

She rolled her eyes. "Let's go the easy route. They use latex gloves in the kitchen." She handed him a pair and put some on herself. Carefully, she lifted the piece of paper from the frame. What if the kidnappers had left a note here, knowing that someone would eventually find it? She couldn't look. "Here, you look." She held it up so he could see the side with the letters and scrunched her eyes closed. "Well, what does it say?" She opened one eye and looked at Cameron.

He studied the paper. Shrugging, he looked up. "The first word is *aksl*. It's a list of words that don't seem to mean anything."

A noise at the door caused them to both turn and look. Emilie, the housekeeper, stood in the doorway. With her French accent, she said, "I am sorry to bother you, Miss Collier, but I saw the door open and wanted to make sure everything was all right."

"Everything is fine. We're looking around."

Emilie looked at the note in Cameron's hand, smiled broadly, and nodded before leaving.

Cameron watched the housekeeper as she walked away. "Odd," he said as she moved out of sight.

Summer shrugged. "Not really. I've never been able to figure her out. Now, about what you said, I agree."

"That's nice, but what are you agreeing to?" The way he smiled as he spoke made her wonder what he had in mind. Had she imagined a slight leer?

"I agree about calling the police."

"I called them when you were gone." He held up the note. "Is there a copy machine around here? The letters are tiny, and I'd like a very clear copy instead of a phone photo."

She grabbed the note. "Excuse me, but did you say you called the police without asking me?" He couldn't have done that. *Stay calm, Summer.*

"Look, I'm sorry. I should have discussed it with you first, but I knew you would agree. Now, is there a copy machine here? An officer could arrive any minute, and I doubt they'll let us make a copy of the note then."

She *would* have agreed. Taking a deep breath, she said, "It's in the office. Follow me." Walking into the lobby, she glanced back and saw Cameron and Cozy look at each other. He seemed sheepish. Did Cozy know something she didn't?

Back in Don's quarters a few minutes later, she tucked the note into the frame while Cameron took off his gloves and put them in his jacket pocket. Just when she had the note settled exactly as they'd found it, she heard an officer in the lobby speaking to Cozy.

Summer and Cameron stood and waited for him. The guilty twinges she felt for taking the note out and looking at it made it feel like hours passed instead of seconds. When they could see the officer through the open door, Cameron poked her in the ribs with his elbow.

"Ouch. What?"

He pointed at her gloves. She whipped her hands behind her back and peeled off the gloves. What did she do with them now? Unfortunately, only one choice came to mind—down the back of her pants.

The missing appointment book may not have interested the police, but the note certainly did. The officer took a photo of it in the frame before carefully removing it with tweezers and slipping it in a plastic bag. "We'll check this for fingerprints."

Cameron smugly smiled at Summer when she glanced at him. She'd have remembered about fingerprints if she hadn't been so excited about the clue.

Sealing the bag, the officer promised to call after their experts had deciphered it, then left.

Summer turned to Cameron. "This is wonderful. We've accomplished so much today. If I'd been alone, I would have given up before I went over that area again. You've been a huge help."

Cameron grinned. "I don't think there's much else for us to accomplish now, so why don't we go home and relax?"

For one breathtaking moment, Summer thought he wanted to relax with her. Then the distracted expression on his face reminded her that he had his own life to lead. "I'm sorry for taking your time like this."

"Don't apologize. I'm helping my sister, remember?"

Summer took a deep breath. She needed to remember that. As they walked outside, she also remembered what the officer had said. She paused at Cameron's truck, shifting from one foot to another.

"Something wrong?"

"Would you mind following me home? This whole thing has made me a little nervous. And the officer who called yesterday said I should be careful."

"No problem." He put the key in his door and opened it. "Will you feel safe in your condo?"

"I'm sure I'll be fine when I'm inside."

He followed her home and idled by the front door until she entered the building. Looking through the glass door, she watched his taillights fade into the distance. Cameron made her feel more secure. How could a stranger make her feel safe and protected?

In her condo, she went straight through to her bedroom to change into PJs. Some serious relaxation was called for, and right now. When she pulled off her pants, the gloves from the inn fell to the ground. Laughing, she picked them up and tossed them overhand into the trash.

After putting on one of her favorite movies, she sat down to unwind. But her thoughts kept going from Don and what terrible things might have happened to him to Cameron acting sweet and kind.

Focusing on the TV, she saw Audrey Hepburn holding onto Gregory Peck as they rode a motor scooter through Rome. She'd missed the first half of the movie.

Cameron would be fun to ride a motor scooter with. She'd wrap her arms around him and hold on tight. A shiver of pleasure shot through her body.

Don needed her.

It was really nice of Cameron to see her home, though.

Shaking her head, she focused on the TV again. Now, Gregory Peck and others were standing before Audrey Hepburn in a palace. She'd missed the whole movie. Hitting the Off button, she got up and went to bed.

Feeling recharged the next morning, a brisk walk through the park sounded like a great way to start the day. Then she'd go to her office. She should be on a weeklong honeymoon, so none of her marketing clients expected her there, and taking the week off was an option. When you owned the business, you *could* do that. But you also knew about lost income when you did. Besides, what else would she do to keep her mind occupied if she didn't work?

A quick change into jeans and a sweatshirt had her outside in minutes. When she looked in front of her, she came back to Earth. Two large men she didn't recognize were standing beside her car. Deep in conversation and clothed in very proper, well-cut business suits, they seemed harmless enough.

She nibbled on her lip. In her year in the condo, she'd never seen anyone stand around in the parking lot. People were always coming or going, but not lingering. Striving for a deliberately casual appearance, she pretended to be interested in the surrounding area and even kicked a pebble as she walked. The men continued their conversation without looking her way, so she took a few more steps.

Halfway to her car, she stopped and put her hand to her mouth. Had she lost her mind? Two men she didn't recognize were standing next to her car, and she had been going to check them out. And she would do what if they *were* after her?

She spun around and hurried back to the building. As she walked, her spine tingled, giving her the sensation that someone watched her from behind. Hastily pushing the door open, she glanced over her shoulder as she entered the building. The men appeared innocent, but that didn't stop her trembling as she sprinted up the stairs to her condo.

Summer grabbed a skirt, jacket, and blouse out of her closet, and pulled them on. Brushing her hair, she walked over to the window and stood there staring at the drapes, not quite able to open them and check outside. Her unit overlooked the parking lot, so she'd have a clear view of her car. By the time she'd gotten up the nerve to look, her hair felt smooth and glossy. She held her breath and gently pulled back the corner of the curtain.

The men were still talking. She dropped the curtain. Who could talk that long? She couldn't.

Even through their engagement, she and Don rarely

spoke for more than five minutes. She preferred to think of them as having shared interests. He truly enjoyed having her work beside him at the inn. Many times, she had left work and gone over there to help him. Giving him a smile over the paperwork encouraged him to reach out and touch her hand. She sighed mistily.

Feet clad in low, navy pumps, she put on her longer wool coat, picked up her purse, and started on her way. If the men looked at her, she'd wave and smile. If they looked friendly, she'd ask them to step away from her car. They didn't look up, so she began the five-block trek to the office.

When she had gone as far as the other side of the parking lot, she stopped and looked back at her car. They had disappeared. So should she take her car or continue walking? Bending over, she looked under the cars to see if anyone had hidden there. Only a harmless robin. Checking between rows as she walked, she reached her car and was driving out of the parking lot in sixty seconds flat.

When she arrived at the building where she leased her office, a dashing older man opened the door to the building. *"Mon petit chou,* we didn't expect to see you this morning."

Summer smiled in spite of the morning she'd had. The majority of the women that made up the female half of this area's retirement community loved Antonio. When he'd first come here to work in security a couple of months ago, he'd instantly become a wonderful welcome to the building.

She smiled more broadly as he smoothed his silver-grey hair and straightened his tie. His face showed the years, but she thought he looked like a movie star from the thirties or forties and suspected others, particularly ladies, agreed. Strangely, he claimed an Italian heritage but mixed words from different languages. Perhaps showmanship ran in the family.

Her friend Ann looked up from the women's clothing shop she managed. "Is this a new look for you, Summer? Not that it isn't interesting," she hurried to add, "but you're normally so conservative."

Summer looked down at her clothes and realized she hadn't paid any attention to what she'd put on. Raising her hands to her cheeks, she felt her skin turn warm. She wore a short, bright-yellow suit jacket over a blue-and-white striped blouse that topped a flirty red-and-black-patterned skirt. She hurried over to a mirror on the shop's wall. The result was . . . she turned to the side . . . bizarre.

Ann and Antonio appeared behind her in the mirror.

"I felt distracted this morning."

"That is understandable with what you've been through, *cherie.*"

Totally embarrassed, Summer said, "Okay, Ann, find me something beautiful to wear."

"Let's see. I received a box of suits this morning. They're just your style, and the color would be beautiful with your brown hair and eyes." She started walking to the back but added, "It's only a partial shipment, so I'll have to see if your size arrived." Ann came out holding a gray jacket and pants that made Summer sigh with relief.

Fifteen minutes later, she stepped out of the dressing room feeling like her old self. She'd even splurged on a new, deep-blue blouse to complete the look.

"You look great. You're good for business." Ann grinned and handed Summer her old clothes in a bag.

"And you're good for the soul. Thanks for disguising

these." She held up the bag. "I wouldn't want anyone else to see them."

Antonio, back at his post, hurried over when she stepped into the lobby. "*Magnifique.*" He picked up her hand and kissed it.

Knowing she looked great—due to Ann's help—she felt self-confidence oozing through her. She could conquer the world. She would find Don. And she would consider marrying him. He'd been hers first, after all. As a woman who ran her own business and had practically run the inn, she felt confident that she could do this without Cameron.

Seated in her office, she leaned back in her chair and smiled. It felt good to be back at work doing what she enjoyed and did well. Feeling daydreamy, she relaxed. Until activity outside her window caught her attention. Then she was ripped out of her daydream and into her new reality.

Across the road and down about half of a block, two men carried on a conversation. Summer studied the men. The clothes were different but their size and coloring were the same. This morning's scene replayed itself before her eyes. She scooted her chair back from the window so they couldn't see her and watched them. Fifteen minutes later, the picture looked the same.

Diving into her work to take her mind off the men, Summer focused on a project that lasted about a half hour. When she finished it, she felt pulled over to the window to look out. The same scene greeted her. She took out another project. This one held her attention for forty-five minutes before she checked the view. Hours passed, but the men remained.

"Want to go to lunch?" a voice asked from behind her.

Summer jumped, then turned to see Ann in her doorway.

"You're a little nervous."

"An officer from the police called Sunday morning and told me to watch out."

"Ooh." Ann spoke sympathetically. "I never thought about you being in danger when Don disappeared. And this must be trying for you, sitting and waiting to hear something."

A second or two passed before Summer understood Ann's meaning. Don could be in grave danger, and she sat here worried about herself. Straightening her shoulders, she said, "Let's go out today. I'd like a break." Summer slipped into her coat. Fumbling with the buttons, she finally gave up and left it open. Looking around carefully as she stepped out the door of the building, she realized that the men were gone and acknowledged that if someone wanted to scare her, they were doing a superb job of it. #

Lunch in a busy, public place helped calm her and, by early afternoon, she felt almost normal. Then two men walked by outside the building. As she reached out to hold onto her desk to steady herself, she noticed one of these men was blond, but both her men had brown hair. These weren't the watchers. She had to solve this mystery and solve it now, or she'd soon be jumping at everything.

Cameron. She had decided not to bother him again, but he seemed to like helping her. Maybe he would have an idea. Before she could change her mind, she picked up the phone and called.

He sounded happy to hear from her. Well, he wasn't groaning. "What can I do for you?" he asked.

Looking at a framed photograph of the Smoky Mountains on her office wall, an idea popped into her mind. "I'm planning to leave the office early. I thought we could go through the inn from top to bottom, examine in and behind everything. We'll see if we can find anything else unusual or suspicious." One painting had given them a possible clue. Maybe others would too.

"That's a great idea, but I can't help tonight."

"Oh." Summer closed her eyes. "I understand. I won't be bothering you again."

"Summer, it isn't what you think. I'm supposed to spend time with my family. John called and talked me into coming by to shoot a few baskets." He paused. "You can join us if you want." From the tone of his voice at the end of the sentence, it sounded like he regretted the offer the moment he'd made it.

No, she wouldn't intrude. "Enjoy yourself. Did you tell the police about Erin?"

Silence met her question. Finally, he said, "I thought about it. You're right. Unless we feel that we have to tell them, I'm not going to. Erin doesn't need this on the front page of the paper. For that matter, neither do you. And you'd be one of two fiancées Don left at the altar."

An image of cameras flashing as she and Erin stood in front of a large photo of Don came into her mind. The story had enough intrigue that it might even be carried nationally. She gulped. "I hadn't thought of it that way. Erin and I both thank you. If you're free tonight after all, I'll be over at the inn, so just call the inn's number. I'm sure you have it."

"Actually, I don't."

Summer thought he hadn't understood the question. "You must have the phone number. Your sister was engaged to Don." Her thoughts wandered in a new direction. "I had never thought about it, but it must have been tricky for him. Don had to manage his schedule with us so we weren't at the inn at the same time."

"She only went to the inn once or twice, and I'd never even seen it until last night. With his business and his home in one location, Don said he liked to get away. Erin has a townhouse in Bellevue and they usually went there."

Summer nodded to herself. Things were starting to make sense. Cozy might have never met Erin.

By four o'clock, she'd gone over the inn's billing and now sat on a stool behind its wooden front desk. Running her finger over the grooves worn by years of use, she thought about solving this mystery alone. Looking for clues would be harder on her own. Two sets of eyes were usually better.

"Summer?"

"Yes?" She looked up.

Cozy put the phone in her hand. "This man says we ordered new brochures, and he needs more information. I don't have a clue."

"I'll do what I can." Taking the phone, she sat down on a couch in the large lobby. The print shop owner frantically described the brochure. Don had missed an appointment to approve the final version for printing. "Can you send me the brochure?" Her phone chimed for the incoming message and she opened the file. "It looks good to me. Print the minimum quantity." She felt movement behind her and turned to see Cameron. He *had* come. Grinning, she beckoned him nearer.

As she set the phone down, she smiled from ear to ear. "Cameron, I'm so glad you're here." Movement beside them startled her. Turning, she found Cozy watching them with an amused expression. Summer added, "I thought you couldn't make it." That should explain her enthusiasm.

Cameron coughed, then spoke. "We rescheduled, and I left work early. Now, you mentioned searching everything, but how can we search rooms when people are in them?"

"Fall and winter are the off-season here, so there usually aren't many guests. When the police cars pulled up and yellow tape went across Don's door, that number dropped significantly."

"I'm surprised anyone is here."

"One regular guest stayed, and some honeymooners have checked in." She started walking toward the stairs. "Of course, the occupied rooms are off limits, but we can still do a thorough search of the rest of the inn."

Upstairs, Cameron rubbed his hands together excitedly. "Let's get started on the search."

When he reached for a painting while she stood in front of him, his fingers brushed her arm. Electricity tingled through her. She had to be able to focus on the search, and she couldn't with him touching her. "How about if I start here and you start over there?" Backing away, she pointed to the other end of the hall.

Summer felt guilty about sending him away, but she missed Don entirely too much when another man could make her tingle. The only problems with that theory, she reminded herself, were that Don never made her tingle and that she'd been planning to call off the wedding.

She removed the painting from the wall and carefully checked for anything, no matter how small, that might be wedged in the frame. Nothing. After rehanging it, she turned around. A young woman in an elegant lace dress stood watching her. She looked as though she'd come from a wedding, and she probably had. The woman continued down the hall, but stopped and watched Cameron as he took a painting off the wall, studied it, and replaced it. Finally, she headed downstairs.

Summer raced over to Cameron. He was staring at a different painting with his head turned sideways.

She leaned her head to the side to see what he did. "This won't work."

He continued to stare at the picture. "What won't work?"

"We have to be more discreet. A guest watched us, and I can't imagine what she thought. If we aren't careful, every guest and employee is going to be taking pictures off the wall and searching them to see what we're looking for."

Standing upright, he gestured at the painting. "What is it?"

"It's an abstract of the inn. I discovered the artist and convinced Don to have it done."

He stepped back and nodded. "I think I see it now."

"Can we get on with it?" She grabbed his arm and tugged. "Now, come on." She pulled on his arm again. "I have an idea."

Down the hall, she opened the utility closet and reached onto a shelf, pulling off a uniform for each of them. "This is about your size. It's a gardener's uniform." She handed him green coveralls. She shrugged and said, "I'm sorry, but that's all we have for men."

"Very sexist."

"Absolutely. But at least we'll look like we belong here." Smiling, she reached onto another shelf. "Here, take this and you'll look even better. And we can help Emilie by dusting as we go."

He looked dubiously at the feather duster in her hand. "I wouldn't know how to use one."

She rolled her eyes. "I don't think it's beyond your capabilities."

Looking abashed, he grinned. "What I mean is—"

She interrupted. "What you mean is, you don't want to figure it out." She glanced around the storeroom. "You need some sort of prop, though."

He reached for a tool chest. "I think this will be suitably masculine."

She nodded with mock seriousness and stepped out the door. "We'll use a couple of empty guest rooms to change, so follow me."

He stopped. "Don't we need keys?"

Smiling, she pulled a ring of keys out of her pocket. "This has been my second home for a while. Don and I work together most evenings." Her smile faded abruptly. She had been having fun just now instead of thinking about how this could be life and death for her fiancé. No matter what he'd done, he didn't deserve that. She felt . . . sympathetic toward him. That surprised her. She could have wrung his neck Saturday night.

She unlocked a guest room door for Cameron. "I'm going to the one next door."

In minutes, Summer, in a black dress with a white apron, carried the previously rejected feather duster over to a hall table. She studied the table's sides and peered under it as she flipped the feathers around.

Cameron checked out a nearby painting. The costumes worked beautifully. A young man, probably the groom, walked past Cameron, nodded a greeting, and went on. Cameron took out tools occasionally and seemed to know what to do with them. He paused with a painting off the wall, pulled out a hammer, and tapped lightly on the wall. When he'd finished with the paintings in the hallway, she signaled for him to come over.

"Anything?" She returned the silk flowers to a vase she'd

just checked inside and out. Then she stepped back to make sure the flowers weren't askew.

"Other than fixing loose picture hangers, no. But we should probably be looking in the rooms too."

She went to the end of the hall and unlocked a door. Wanting to keep things friendly but formal, she spoke in her most businesslike tone. "Why don't you try the room on the end and I'll finish here?"

Double-checking to make sure they hadn't missed anything in the hall, she soon went into the guest room where Cameron was working. He pulled dresser drawers completely out, examined the bottoms and sides of them, and put them back.

Puzzled, she asked, "What are you doing?"

"I thought a clue could be somewhere other than tucked in a frame. A folded piece of paper doesn't take much room. And I'm sure I saw someone in a detective show hide something by taping it under a drawer."

"It's a good idea." She nodded. "Did you search the nightstand?"

"I've only done this side of the room, so not yet."

She removed a nightstand's drawer and turned it over. It just looked like the bottom of a drawer. Silently working side by side, they made their way around the room. After inspecting the closet and drapes, Summer stripped the bed. "I know the classic place to hide something is between the mattress and box spring. Can you help me lift this?"

Cameron turned while holding onto a pillow from the wingback chair. "Huh? You want me to help you with the bed?"

She felt steamy just hearing him say the word "bed." He

lifted the mattress as she directed. When she'd checked under it, he set it down.

"Thanks. I think I'll be done with this side of the room when I get the linens back on the bed. How about you?"

"I've finished looking in, under, and around the furniture. I saw you check out the drapes, right?"

She laughed. "Considering that I stood behind them for at least five minutes, going over every inch, yes, you're right."

He grinned back. "I'll get started on the room next door."

Concentrating on her task, Summer held up the key ring, and he took it from her. About fifteen seconds passed before she realized what he'd said. Oh no! The room next door was the only occupied room on this end of the hall, and the guests were honeymooners. They wouldn't answer a knock on the door. Honeymooners rarely did.

She raced out of the room and found him quietly backing out the door of the other room. He jumped when he turned and found her there. Then he put his finger to his lips to shush her. After gently closing the door, he leaned against it and set the tool chest on the floor.

She bit her lip to keep from bursting into laughter.

He glared at her. "Your eyes are laughing."

She nodded and took a deep breath. Still biting her lip, she managed to say, "Sorry, honeymooners. Were they . . . ?"

He breathed a huge sigh of relief. "No, they were sleeping, wrapped in each other's arms."

Summer felt herself blush at the image he'd painted. Pushing it aside, she squared her shoulders. They had a search to continue. "Only one other room is occupied right now, and it's at the opposite end of the hall."

"Good. Are you done with that room?" He pointed at the one they'd just left.

"I have to finish making the bed. You go on to the next one."

He looked at her skeptically.

Summer smiled. "It's safe. Another honeymoon suite, but unoccupied." He raised his eyebrows and didn't move, so she said, "How about if I go first?"

"That sounds like a winning idea."

She inserted the key in the lock and started to turn the knob. Stopping, she wondered if she'd misread the guest list. She pushed the door open slowly, her eyes looking right at the bed. It was untouched. What a relief.

Summer pointed inside. "Get going."

When he started through the door, she put her hand on his arm and pointed at the floor where he'd been standing. "Can't have a man without a tool chest."

He laughed and reached for it. Inside, Cameron pointed toward the center of the room. "What's that?"

"A large, heart-shaped bathtub." She walked over to it and looked inside. "Filled with water. Romantic pink rose petals are sprinkled in the water and around the edge. If I remember correctly, honeymooners booked this suite before everything happened with Don. I guess the couple cancelled because they didn't want criminals around while they honeymooned."

Cameron had walked up behind her while she spoke. "Rose petals?" He laughed.

"Have you no romance in you?"

"I have just as much romance as the next man. But pink rose petals must have been a woman's idea."

"It's part of the honeymoon package. And yes, I thought of it." She knelt down in the middle of the rose petals that lay on the edge of the tub and reached to open the drain. As her knee started to slide toward the water, she grabbed for the faucet.

"Do you need help?"

Chuckling, Summer said, "I'd thought I was going in the drink for a minute." She let go of the faucet, reached again to open the drain, and felt herself slipping on a rose petal. Instantly, she became airborne. "Help!" she cried.

CHAPTER SIX

$\mathcal{H}$eadfirst in the bath, she fought to get her head up. Cameron's arms wrapped around her and lifted her to a sitting position in the water. Sputtering, she opened her eyes.

"Are you okay?"

Blinking, she rubbed her eyes. "Soggy but good."

He kneeled beside the tub, grinning. Then he reached down to give her a hand up.

Summer stared at him. "Not going to say anything?"

"Not a word. Well, maybe just a few. You have a rosy complexion." He reached over and plucked a rose petal off her ear. He offered her his hand again. "Ready to get out?"

She looked at his hand for a moment. "Think this is funny, huh?"

He nodded. She took his hand and tugged to throw him off balance. As he flew through the air, she pressed herself to the side of the tub to give him room to land. Rose petals sprayed the air when he hit the water. Seconds later, he sat upright in the water.

Laughing, they sat side by side. Summer stared at him. He was so . . . nice. He gently touched her cheek as he brushed the hair off her face, and it rocked her to her soul.

Coming to her feet, she stepped out of the water. Summer Collier definitely wasn't in the market for another man.

Focusing on something, anything else, she said, "The petals have been in there long enough to scent the water." She pushed a rose petal off her eyelid and blew the water off her lips.

"Yeah. It's lovely."

His sarcasm made her laugh. "You think so?" Summer grinned at him. "Let's get out of here."

Chuckling, Cameron leaned back in the tub. "Summer, you're a rose from head to toe." She looked down. Rose petals covered her body. "A rose by any other name would smell as sweet."

"Stop!" She covered her ears with her hands. She reached for a bath towel and threw it at Cameron. As it hit him in the head, Cozy walked into the room.

Summer stilled. "I leaned over to open the drain but slipped and fell in."

Cozy stared at Cameron. "And him?"

Summer shrugged. "He laughed at me, so I pulled him in."

"I'm so happy to see you smiling. You'd become more and more wooden."

Summer knew she'd been driven since Don had disappeared, so that must have been what Cozy meant. Looking at Cameron, she smiled. "But he smells lovely now."

Cozy laughed. "Well, I'll leave you two alone. Mr. Breznowski asked for additional towels, so I was coming to get some." She left with a glance over her shoulder and a chuckle.

As Summer dried herself off, Cameron got out of the bath and picked up a towel for himself. She wrapped her head turban-style with another towel before walking toward the door. "I'm going for another set of uniforms for us. I'll be right back."

They had taken turns changing in the bathroom and were sitting on the suite's couch, relaxing for a minute, when Cozy returned. "Now that you're dry, I'm going to ask: why the uniforms? What's going on?"

Summer and Cameron looked at each other.

"She's trustworthy," Summer said.

"Trustworthy? Is this about Mr. Daily?"

Summer nodded. "Sit down. It's a long story."

Summer left out the part about Erin. She would protect the woman as long as she could without lying.

Cozy shook her head when she'd been brought up to date. "Maybe we should look everything over in case we find a clue somewhere else."

"We are."

"I spend more time upstairs than you do, Summer, so let me look around too. The restaurant's been slow lately. I can have Ricardo, one of the waiters, fill in at the front desk."

Summer smiled. "Let's do it." Touching the towel on her head, she added, "Just as soon as I dry my hair."

Later, when they walked near the honeymoon suite Cameron had entered by mistake, Cozy put out her arm to stop him.

"Don't worry. I warned him earlier." Summer looked over at Cameron, and he blushed.

They went from room to room, looking through everything until Cozy stopped at a table in room 221 and closely examined the lamp that sat on it. "This isn't the lamp that sat here before."

"What? Are you sure?" Summer picked up the lamp and looked it over. "It certainly is beautiful. I've always loved these Tiffany-style lamps."

"I'm sure. I pay attention to the details. You know how Mr. Daily is about the little things, so I think of it as part of my job." She tapped her foot. "This had to be new in the last month or so."

Cameron carefully took the lamp from Summer. "Why the last month?"

"We were so busy getting ready for a large wedding at the inn that I didn't have time to pay attention."

"I wonder if this is a genuine antique. We could search online, but the library downstairs may have something on antiques." Summer asked.

"I'm sure there must be." Cozy ran down the stairs and, puffing from exertion, came back a few minutes later with her arms full of books. "Here." She tossed them on the bed.

They each took a book and sat down.

"Find the section on Tiffany lamps," Cameron directed.

When they finished reading, they crowded around the lamp. Summer searched for each of the indicators her book had mentioned regarding the genuine versus the copy and found them. "Whew! This lamp might be valuable. According to the book, it would be worth a small fortune. Cozy knows it's new to the inn, so it can't be from the inn's previous owners. That means Don must have bought it."

Cozy burst out laughing. Then she put her hand over her mouth and appeared uncomfortable. "I'm sorry, Summer, but you know Mr. Daily wouldn't spend money on a genuine antique."

Summer had to agree. "I guess you're right."

Cameron grinned. "Cheap, huh?"

Summer gave him a haughty glare. "Conservative with his money." After putting the lamp back on the table, she studied it. "We need to take it to an expert and find out for sure."

The bell on the front door jingled faintly in the distance, and Cozy sighed. "I have to go back to work now. Ricardo only knows so much." She looked at them hopefully. "You will tell me what happens, though, right?"

"Of course. We wouldn't have paid any attention to this lamp without you."

Cozy hurried out the door.

Cameron tossed his book on the bed. "Now, back to the business at hand. Considering the attention someone has given Don's quarters, maybe we shouldn't take this out of here to get it appraised. That someone might be watching."

Shrugging, she looked at him. "But what else can we do?"

"An expert can come here."

"Great idea, Cameron, but who would do that?"

"Frank Semple from Semple Antiques."

Summer laughed. "Even I've heard of him. He's the owner of the most exclusive antique shop in the South." She raised an eyebrow. "I don't think he'd want to come all the way over here to look at one lamp."

Cameron sat on the edge of the bed and crossed his arms over his chest. "He would for a friend."

Summer plopped down beside him, excited at the prospect. "You know Frank Semple?" She went on without waiting for an answer, "Oh, this is fabulous. His expert opinion will tell us what we have." She lay back on the bed. "But I'm sure it's a wonderful copy. Cozy's right. Don wouldn't have any real antiques here."

He watched her lying on the bed. "It's hard for me to believe that you are a professional who owns a successful marketing firm."

Summer sat up and straightened and smoothed her hair back with her hand. "Because I don't look like a professional now?"

"Because you're so approachable. You don't dress or act like the marketing powerhouse that I know you are."

She stared at him. "It sounds like you've been doing more research on me."

"I asked around."

She felt . . . flattered. "I do have my elegant moments. You should have seen me in my wedding dress." She groaned. "Wait, you did see me in my wedding dress. But not at my peak. I looked better a few hours earlier." She laughed. Cameron had been good for her soul.

He put his arms around her and gently held her.

"Hi, all." When Cozy walked into the room, Summer pushed Cameron away and walked over to study the lamp. Cozy blinked a couple of times. Then she backed toward the door. "Sorry, carry on." Grinning, she pulled the door closed behind herself.

"Now what must she be thinking?" Summer asked.

Cameron sat on the edge of the bed. "I know what's she's thinking."

"We're friends and you were holding me for comfort. I'll explain it to her later. She'll understand." While pretending to study the lamp, she changed the subject. "I hope finding out about this lamp will bring us closer to finding Don."

Cameron mumbled something under his breath, stomped to a chair, and sat down. He dialed his friend, and she could hear the conversation enough to know that Frank would be over shortly. After changing back into their own clothes, they sat in the lobby and waited. She glanced at Cameron. Why had he held her, and why had she let him? She was an engaged woman. Sort of.

Frank arrived very quickly. A man of his reputation had to be busy, so Cameron must be a good friend.

Back in room 221, Frank dragged the room's only chair in front of the lamp. He carefully examined it, turning it and studying it from every angle, while Summer sat beside Cameron on the bed. Then Frank stood and paced around the room. He paused briefly to stare at the lamp but soon resumed his pacing.

Cameron jumped off the bed. "Well, Frank?"

Frank stopped his pacing. "Impatient as always, huh?"

Summer watched the men. Cameron, impatient? That added an interesting twist to his personality. Cameron was sweet, kind, gentle, and intelligent. So many wonderful qualities. But she didn't want another man in her life now. Superhero or not.

Frank sat in the chair. Staring at the lamp, he said, "It's genuine."

"Are you sure?" Cameron walked over and picked up the lamp.

"Careful." Frank held his hands to catch it if it fell.

"You handle antiques all the time, Frank. Why are you so worried about this one?"

"This lamp is worth a fortune."

Cameron slowly set it on the table and stepped back.

Summer walked over. "That can't be. Unless," she said, looking at Frank, "Don, the owner of the inn, bought it and didn't know its true value. You see that kind of thing on the evening news when it happens."

Frank shook his head. "I doubt it, but it is possible. Let me do some research." He looked longingly at the lamp. "Do you think the owner will want to sell it?"

Summer answered, "Probably. It sounds like Don can make a lot of money on it, so I doubt he will want to keep it. I'll talk to him when we find him."

"Find him?" Frank looked at the two of them.

"He's my fiancé and has been missing since we were supposed to be married last Friday."

Frank looked from one to the other. "I thought that you two were—"

Cameron grabbed his arm and pulled him to the door.

Summer could see them talking then Frank looked back at her and laughed. What could they be saying?

As Frank walked away, Cameron came back into the room. "He says he'll call in a couple of days. Now, how about having dinner in the restaurant downstairs? I'm hungry."

She wanted to know what they'd said but knew it would be futile to ask. One thing she'd learned: Cameron could keep a secret with the best of them.

Summer stretched and yawned. Then she rolled over and checked the time. Eight thirty! She liked to be in her office by nine. Throwing back the covers, she pulled on her robe and hurried toward the kitchen, walking through a warm pool of sunlight in front of the window. Feeling dreamy, she listened to chirping birds. Mornings were so serene and peaceful.

Vroom. Vroom. A car revved its engine. *Vroom. Vroom.* It sounded like a race car would plow through her wall any second. Groggy, she stumbled over to the window and pulled back the curtain. A man was leaning over the engine on a car in the parking lot, just two cars away from hers. Another man sat behind the wheel, pressing the accelerator. He stepped out and went over to the repairman, who stood and talked to him.

When she could see both faces, she jumped back and dropped the curtain. The men were back. What should she do?

Vroom. Vroom. The revving continued.

Putting her hands over her ears, she tried to block out the sound, but it barely helped. She wouldn't be able to hear the vehicle in the shower, so she would be able to think more clearly there.

Steamy, hot water spraying down, she stepped into the shower stall. As the minutes passed, she felt more and more rational. So what if she'd seen them here twice? They were just two men. Large men, but just two men.

An answer came to her. The men had moved into one of the condos. They were her new neighbors. She'd seen them near her office, but that could be a coincidence.

Happy with her simple solution, Summer shut off the water, then reached out and rooted around on the shelf for a towel. Her hand brought back the only thing left—a washcloth. Looking down at it, a grin twitched at one corner of her mouth. It wouldn't do much. She wiped her face with it and tossed it to the side. Running the laundry became more of a need each day and less of an option. She'd have to make time during her search for Don to take care of the ordinary.

Groaning, she pulled her robe over her wet body, then, dripping across the floor, went to the phone and called the building manager. A minute later, she slowly set down the phone. No one had moved in recently.

When she looked out the window, she saw the manager walking across the parking lot to the men. They gestured at the car. He smiled and walked back. A knock sounded on her door a few minutes later.

"Yes?" she called through the closed door.

"Miss Collier, the men say they needed to fix their car, so they pulled into the parking lot. They should be done in a minute."

"Thank you." She heard footsteps going away and leaned her forehead against the door. Unlike the manager, she knew they'd parked their car here before. And both days, they'd been near her car. Since they'd appeared right after Don disappeared, she had to conclude that they were here to watch her.

Now she had a problem. If she walked out to her car to drive to work, the men might come after her. And if she walked to work, the men might come after her.

She called a taxi. By the time the taxi pulled in front of the door to the building, the men were gone. The cabbie drove away with a great tip, and Summer drove herself to work.

Her morning in the office went well. A new client called. She set an appointment to meet with him and his management team at their offices in Atlanta in three weeks. Her life had to be back to normal in three weeks.

Ann popped in at eleven thirty. "I'll go get us some lunch. You want your usual?"

"Yes, a turkey sandwich, no mayo."

Instead of launching into a large project, Summer took care of some filing she'd been meaning to do. Done, she walked over to the windows. Another beautiful, sunny day. When she saw Ann walk out of the deli carrying two white bags, she took a couple of cans of soda out of her little fridge. A few minutes later, her friend rounded the corner to Summer's office.

Summer quickly unwrapped her sandwich and took a bite. "Yum."

"They do make a great sandwich." Ann watched as Summer took another bite. "You must be hungry."

"I only had a muffin and tea earlier, but I usually eat a large breakfast."

"Does Don like a big breakfast too?" Ann took a bite of her sandwich.

Summer suddenly found the corner of her sandwich fascinating. "I don't know."

Ann made choking sounds and reached for her bottle of soda. "You were engaged for . . ."

"Three months," Summer supplied.

"And you don't know," Ann paused, "his taste in breakfast?"

"You know I was waiting for marriage. But I have to say the question never needed to be answered. Don didn't seem interested in that sort of thing."

Ann shook her head and took another bite. "I have a husband who loves breakfast."

Summer laughed. "I'm glad your needs are met. But there are more important things."

"Such as?"

"Enjoying each other's company."

"And you enjoy being with him?"

Summer's mind wandered to the time she had spent with Cameron, but she pushed the thought away. "Yes, I like being with Don."

Her watch showed a few minutes before two when the

client she'd asked about Cameron and his architectural reputation dropped by.

"Samantha Martin, it's great to see you. Come in."

The woman floated into the room on a cloud of French perfume. "I thought you might have an opening this after-noon since you're supposed to be on your honeymoon." The woman gracefully lowered herself to the chair.

Summer winced, and the other woman caught her expression.

"I shouldn't have said that. I apologize. Please don't take it out on the quality of your work."

Summer laughed. Samantha Martin had such a likable way about her. "What is the project?"

"I'm going to take tour groups to the fashion houses in France and Italy. I'd like for you to handle marketing."

"This sounds fun!"

Ms. Martin smiled indulgently and leaned forward. "That's what you bring to your work that your competitors don't. We're going to start with three ten-day tours in the next year. We'll be flying out of New York, so promote it all over the East and South."

Summer's mind whirred. This could make her name in the business.

Her client continued, "I have an idea. My team and I are taking the tour ourselves in about six weeks as a trial run. Why don't you come with us? It's my gift to you. You'll return the expense with brilliant marketing concepts based on the places you've visited."

Summer thought about it for all of a second. "I'd love to!"

The woman rose as elegantly as she'd lowered herself into the chair. "How is Mr. Cameron Powers? I brushed into him once at a dinner for something or other. Whew. Made me want to get to know him better. There's something about that man. And he's talented too."

"Yes, I saw his house."

She raised her eyebrows. "Did you? Have you met his family?"

"Two brothers."

The woman slowly nodded. "Cameron Powers is very private about his family and his home. You're one in a thousand." She left with a speculative look on her face.

Summer stood at her office window and watched her leave. As her luxury car pulled onto the street, Summer thought about the other woman's expression and laughed. To meet his family and see his house, you simply had to step on his cat and climb his tree.

She spent her afternoon creating interesting ideas for the tour of fashion houses. After that, she sat in her office humming while she looked through her client list and made notes of what she needed to accomplish for each one. Pausing her humming, she thought of the men she kept finding nearby.

Maybe seeing them so many times was coincidental. Nashville had a lot of visitors. Perhaps they were tourists and already on their way home. Ideally to somewhere thousands of miles away. That thought made her quite happy.

And the Tiffany lamp might even have a logical explanation. Don had probably bought it at a secondhand store for a few dollars. That just left her with a runaway groom, a second bride, and the rooms that had been ransacked.

To get away from the situation, she decided to go to the mall after work. Her favorite department store was having a sale. Shopping and a sale—what a fabulous combination.

By four thirty, she had begun to think about wrapping up

her pleasant day at work. When she heard someone coming upstairs, she didn't even look up. It would be Ann. They often walked out to their cars together and chatted about men and life.

She looked up when Ann spoke, "Summer, someone's here to see you."

Cameron stood in her doorway. She couldn't prevent a smile.

Ann looked from one to the other and got an expression on her face that Summer ignored. Ann stepped outside the door, but Summer knew curiosity would have her friend watching and listening from nearby. She didn't want to close the door on Ann, though. It would be fine. She had nothing to hide, after all. *If you don't count almost everything that's happened in my life during the last week.*

Cameron walked over, leaned close, and spoke in a whisper, "Frank called."

Her forehead wrinkled in puzzlement. She answered in normal tones, "He said he would call."

He looked exasperated and whispered, "But he has unexpected information for us and wants to meet us at the inn later tonight."

"Fine," she whispered back. "Why the secrecy? And why didn't you simply call and tell me?"

"I had to drive over here anyway to meet Frank, so I thought I'd come early."

Summer saw Ann watching them and called out to her, "Ann, come meet my friend, Cameron."

Ann had a sheepish expression when she entered the room. She walked over and shook his hand. "Pleased to meet any friend of Summer's. I'd better run back downstairs."

When they were alone, Cameron said, "Also, I was worried about you."

He didn't even know about the two men who might be following her. "Why?"

He looked at her like she was clueless. Then he ticked off the reasons on his fingers. "Your fiancé is missing. Someone trashed his quarters. Then, we discovered a mysterious note behind a picture and a valuable antique."

She'd forgotten about the note.

He continued, "Something strange is going on and you're in the middle of it." He sat on the edge of her desk. "I don't want you going anywhere alone. I thought we could go together to the inn."

Really? How arrogantly male of him. "I have an errand to run after work, but you can come with me. I'll even let you drive. We can leave when I've finished my work. Make yourself comfortable for about a half hour." Thirty-five minutes later, she stood up and smiled. "Well, come on then. We're going shopping."

CHAPTER SEVEN

"*D*o you really have to shop in this department?" Cameron furtively scanned the area. He probably wanted to see if anyone he knew was watching. It wasn't likely. Cameron was the lone man in the cosmetics department.

"What do you think?" Summer held up another tube of lipstick and read the label. "This one's called Pink Passion." He had been so overbearing with his decision to look after her that she wanted to pay him back and thought her plan was working. They'd been to three counters where she'd tried on eye shadow, blush, and numerous lipsticks. He'd been uncomfortable since they entered the department.

Cameron stared longingly at the lipstick. "It would be incredibly sexy . . . on you." He looked at her lustfully.

Oh no! She hadn't planned on this. The tube fell out of her hand onto the counter. Her plan had backfired. What did one do with a lipstick-aroused man?

Cameron picked up a tube of lip gloss. "It's called Delight.

Yes." He lowered his voice and looked into her eyes. "You'd be delightful wearing it."

Summer's heart raced. What now?

After a moment of silence, Cameron burst out laughing.

Summer smacked his arm. "Arrgh. You knew I was torturing you."

"Of course."

"I'm ready to go."

"But you didn't buy anything, and they're having a sale. You said you love a sale."

"I'll come back another time." Summer looked around. Makeup stared at her from all directions, but Cameron's expression had taken away her interest in shopping. She'd like for him to look at her like that and mean it.

What was she thinking? A few weeks ago, she'd been finalizing the details for her wedding. Now, another man occupied her mind day and night. *Think of something else.* Honeymoon. She could have been on her honeymoon in a beautiful place right now. Maybe somewhere exotic. Frugal with his money, Don probably hadn't chosen a private island, but she had still hoped for a special destination.

Something touched her arm. "Summer?"

She jumped. "Huh?"

"We're in front of the mall. Where were you?"

She looked up at the mall sign. "Oh, I was on my honeymoon."

He gave her an odd look.

"I meant to say that our honeymoon location might be an important clue to Don's whereabouts."

He frowned. "He took the secret of the honeymoon destination with him."

Pursing her lips, she thought it over. "Maybe there's something in his office. No. I have a better idea." She clapped her hands together. "Why didn't I think of this before? He probably chose the same travel agent he used for business trips. I'll call them."

Cameron looked at his watch. "It's six thirty. They're closed by now."

"Nope. I've called them in the evening for both guests and Don." She pulled her cell phone out of her purse and glanced around.

"What are you looking for?"

"A place to sit and call."

"Maybe the bench beside you will work."

Summer glared at him. "Do they teach sarcasm in architect school? You're very good at it."

He smiled. "No, it's a gift."

Smiling back, she sat down with her phone and called. The owner was happy to help, but, a couple of minutes later, Summer stood and put the phone back in her purse with no helpful information to report. "They didn't have a reservation for the honeymoon, and the police had already called to check."

"We should have realized they would check all angles. They've probably looked through his office for clues too."

She nodded. "I'll think of something. I want to find him."

Cameron looked distracted as they walked to his car. He unlocked his door, got inside, and closed it behind him. Fingers tapping the steering wheel, he seemed deep in thought. After a minute of standing at the passenger door, she knocked on the window. He jumped, then unlocked the door.

"Planning to leave me here?" She dropped her purse between the seats.

"Sorry." He sheepishly glanced over at her.

"Could we drop by my apartment for a minute? I'd like to put on something more comfortable."

"After that stunt you pulled in the cosmetics department, I should answer that it would help to arrive at the inn early, and it might. But we've got the time."

Feeling her face grow warm, she said, "You were high-handed about protecting me. I know you meant well."

He surprised her by sitting back and laughing.

An image of him holding onto the tube of lipstick appeared in her mind. He hadn't even been mad about their little tour through the cosmetics department.

"I was very male, wasn't I? I'm used to protecting Erin. Sorry."

She smiled. "Apology accepted. She must be different than I am."

"She is." He started his truck and pulled out, adding, "But please be careful."

"I always am. And I do like having you around."

He turned and looked at her. Ooh, she didn't want him to get the wrong idea. "You've been very helpful on your sister's behalf," she added.

When they pulled into her condo's parking lot, Cameron parked the truck. He turned toward her and appeared to be staring right into her soul, seeking an answer to a question. Finally, he glanced down at his watch. "Wow. We'd better hurry." He popped open his truck door and stepped to the ground. "I don't want Frank to have to wait."

In her condo, Summer hurried through to her bedroom to change. "Make yourself a cup of tea, if you'd like."

"Yuck."

"What?" She put her head out the door.

"I know you're going to be surprised, but I don't like tea."

She went back into her room and closed the door. "There's some instant coffee in the cupboard."

"Also yuck."

She answered through the closed door as she pulled clothes out. "Coffee snob?"

"I wouldn't use the word 'snob.' Let's just say that instant coffee isn't real coffee."

She laughed as she pulled a sweater over her head. With jeans and comfortable shoes on, she joined him in her living room. She prepared tea and put it in a travel mug.

"I've been considering any and all clues. I know Erin's in Hawaii at her honeymoon destination. Did Don give you any clues about the location of yours?"

"Only that the place had similar weather to here."

"The weather clue does exclude a good portion of the world. Nothing else?"

"Nothing that I can think of. And believe me, I asked a lot of questions. I told him that to pack appropriately, I needed to know the climate. So he told me. Beyond that, he just said he wanted to surprise me." She looked at the mantel clock. "We'd better be going. Speaking of clues, did Frank tell you why he wanted to see us?" She locked the apartment door as they left, and they went to his truck.

"He left a brief and concise message that said to meet him there." He shrugged. "But he's like that."

"How do you know him?"

He carefully backed the truck out and started for the inn. "We were getting master's degrees at the same time and seemed to run in the same circles. We ended up being friends."

"It must be nice to have friends here. I'm from a place that's more than a thousand miles away. I went to college there too. I have lots of friends. There."

"What made you move here?"

"My parents retired here. When I came to visit a year ago, I didn't want to leave. It's a city, but not too big, and the people are friendly. So I went home, packed up, and moved here."

Cameron pulled into the inn's driveway and past the *1902 Inn* sign. Just a week ago, she had felt warm and fuzzy when she saw that sign. Like she'd come home.

"Your parents live here? Why haven't I seen them during this fiasco with Don?"

"They're traveling through Thailand and won't be back until close to Christmas. They love going to remote areas, so I haven't heard from them in a while. Don wouldn't wait until December for the wedding because the inn is too busy during the holidays."

"Thoughtful man," he muttered.

She glared at him. "He is."

Cozy rushed over to them when they walked in the door. She leaned close and whispered, "Mr. Semple is upstairs. Does he know any more about you-know-what?"

"Why don't you come and see for yourself?" Cameron asked.

Cozy put her hand on her forehead and took a dramatic pose. "Alas, no. This is the busy time."

Summer laughed, and Cameron looked startled. She reached for his arm and pulled him along. "Theater major." She gestured back at Cozy.

"That explains a lot."

"What does that mean?" Cozy loudly asked as they climbed the stairs.

"Great hearing too." He looked over at the front desk. "It means that you have a style that is distinctly your own. You know, you'd be perfect for my stuffed-shirt younger brother, John."

"If he looks like you, bring him around."

Cameron surprised Summer by blushing. She felt something like jealousy about the easy relationship Cozy and Cameron seemed to be developing, but she squelched that immediately. Jealousy was a useless emotion. Beyond that, she had no right to feel anything more than friendship toward Cameron.

They entered the guest room and found Frank once again sitting in the chair in front of the lamp, staring at it. He turned the lamp a bit and focused intently on one area. Then turned it again and stared at another area. She expected him to pull out a magnifying glass soon.

Cameron sat on the bed. Summer looked dubiously at the bed, then longingly at the chair that Frank sat on. Seeing no alternative, she shrugged and sat beside Cameron.

"Find anything interesting, Frank?"

Frank jumped out of the chair. "Whew, you scared me."

"Why so jumpy?" Cameron leaned forward to rest his elbows on his knees.

Frank walked over to the doorway and peered out and around the hall before closing and locking the door.

Cameron pointed to the chair. "Sit. You're making *me* jumpy."

After Frank had paced back and forth a couple of times, Cameron got up and pushed him into the chair. "Now, talk."

The antiques expert inhaled and exhaled deeply before glancing over at the lamp. "I've done a great deal of research, and I discovered something I've never come across before."

Summer walked over and knelt in front of the lamp. "It's a copy, isn't it?"

Frank ran his hand over his face and stood. "No, it's a genuine Tiffany lamp."

She stood. "Really? Then what's the problem?"

Frank turned and looked at both of them. "It's stolen."

"Stolen?" Cameron shouted.

"Shh," Frank looked heavenward.

The three of them paced the room, stopping occasionally as if to speak, then silently continuing. Finally, Summer paused and looked around. They looked like something out of a bad movie. She put out her hands to stop the others.

"We have no choice but to call the police," Frank said.

Summer walked over to the lamp. "But what if they think we're involved and come to arrest us?"

"Why would they think that?" Frank asked.

"Summer's fiancé vanishes. The missing man's home is ransacked. A stolen lamp suddenly appears. It could appear suspicious. That she's"—Cameron pointed at Summer—"the guilty party."

Summer stared at her feet. She should tell Cameron about the two men who were following her. They might be the lamp thieves. But she wouldn't tell him right now. She'd wait until Frank left. They didn't need to get the antiques expert more involved in this than he'd already become.

Cameron seemed to have a similar idea. "Thank you, Frank. We can take care of things from this point."

Frank seemed to hesitate a moment. He set a printed page on the table. "Here is all the information I could find. Maybe it will help." He opened the door and paused. "And let me know if I can find any more information for you."

They nodded, and he left. Then they looked at each other.

Summer walked over and sat in the chair Frank had vacated. "He's right. We should call the police." She studied the lamp. "This is so beautiful that I'm not surprised it's genuine."

"You've been involved in this mystery from the beginning. The police may suspect you have something to do with it. Maybe Don knew about the lamp and ran because of it. Maybe you knew about it, too, but thought you could sell it."

How could Cameron think she had anything to do with it? After everything they'd been through together, did he really think she was a thief? Summer stood, fuming with anger. "Mr. Powers, I appreciate the help you have given me, but I never want to see you again." She ran for the door, but he caught her arm as she went by.

"I was giving you the law enforcement scenario." He pulled her close, and she stopped struggling against him. "I know you're innocent."

She rested against him and soaked in the comfort. "Maybe we should keep trying to solve this ourselves." She looked up at him. "And, if we haven't solved it soon, we go to the police?"

"What can we do that the police haven't already done?"

Summer turned to Cameron with tears in her eyes. They had to *do* something. She pulled away and sat in the chair.

Cameron knelt in front of her. "You know Don better than anyone, so perhaps you know something and don't even realize it." He snapped his fingers. "I know. Maybe he's hiding in a favorite place. Where did you like to go together?"

Summer bowed her head and thought over the time she'd known Don. "We talked about this before. I always came here." There had to be more to their relationship than the inn. *Think, Summer. Think!* Nothing came to mind. Sighing, she said, "We went out to eat. That's it."

For some odd reason, Cameron seemed pleased by her response. "Speaking of dinner, why don't we see about eating in the restaurant downstairs? I enjoyed it the other night."

She walked with him to the door. "You did notice the curious looks, though, didn't you? You were eating with the boss' fiancée."

"You're right. There were a few uncomfortable moments. Do you know of anywhere else around here?"

"How about Mama Maria's?"

Later, when she'd finished her lasagna, she sat back and smiled. He'd opted for spaghetti and meatballs tonight.

He waved her hand away when she reached for the check. "You paid at the inn."

Summer silently watched him pay the check. As they stood, she grinned and said, "They don't charge me at the inn. But thank you for dinner anyway."

Leaving the restaurant, Cameron glanced back toward the tables.

"What is it?" She looked over her shoulder.

"It's strange, but I thought I saw those two men at the mall." He stopped and pointed at a table across the room.

The two men were just finishing their salads. Summer felt the world going dim. Taking deep breaths, she moved toward the door. "Let's get out of here." The exit slowly got closer.

"Not until you tell me what this is all about." He spoke from where he stood.

"I promise to tell you, but let's leave. Now."

Her legs finally worked normally, so she hurried out the door with Cameron chasing behind her.

In his truck, she confessed about the men. "I know I should have told you"—she held up her hand at the protest she knew he was about to make—"but I wanted it to be a coincidence. I hadn't seen them in two days, so I hoped they were visitors to Nashville and had gone home." Resting her elbow against the door, she added, "I guess they became better at hiding."

"They were in plain sight in the restaurant."

"Yes, but I was only looking at you." Summer sat up and clamped her hand over her mouth. "I meant that while we talked, I wasn't paying attention to my surroundings." She glanced surreptitiously at him, but he didn't appear to have noticed the suggestive note to her words.

By the time they reached her condo, Cameron had a plan. "Tomorrow, we should check everything at the inn again to make sure nothing else is hidden there. And, if I remember the schedule, Cozy will be there, so she can help us."

Summer opened the door and stepped to the ground. "You remember correctly. Should I meet you there?"

He agreed and drove off.

The next day at the office went quickly. She left a half hour early and rushed home. As she put her key in the door, she thought about getting ready to see Cameron. Laughing at herself, she turned the key. "I'm getting ready to look for clues to find Don," she said firmly.

Changed into jeans, a long-sleeved T-shirt, and a sweater, she sat on the bed to put on her shoes and socks. Maybe she should get away from everything and go to her special place in the woods. A short hike and some time spent relaxing beside a babbling brook would help her unwind. She could lose the two men and enjoy herself. She paused with one sock on. The men hadn't gotten so good at following her that they'd be able to walk soundlessly through the woods, had they? She laughed and slipped on the other sock. Daniel Boone wasn't chasing her. She'd definitely consider getting away to the forest.

Who were these men anyway? They must be working for the criminal who had kidnapped Don. If they kidnapped her, they would probably expect her to tell them something. But she didn't have anything *to* tell. Someone had ransacked Don's quarters before the men started following her. Maybe they wanted whatever that *someone* had been searching for there.

Cameron agreed with her conclusions when she met him at the inn a short time later. Unfortunately, several people stood at the front desk, and the phone was ringing. Cameron shrugged as he watched the scene. "It's too busy for Cozy to get away, and I don't know how helpful it will be if you and I search alone again."

Summer agreed. "Why don't I sit in for Cozy, and the two of you can search."

"I'd rather you came along." He paused. "But your idea makes sense."

They walked over and told Cozy the plan, which she happily agreed to.

An hour later, Summer was tapping her fingers on the front desk and her feet on the rung of the wooden stool she perched on. The constant stream of patrons had finally let up, and restlessness was setting in. Looking around the room, she contemplated sneaking away.

No one was in the lobby. Maybe she could just go to the

top of the stairs and see if she could spot Cameron or Cozy. As she got to her feet, the entrance opened and two dark-haired men walked in the door.

She dropped down behind the front desk. Shaking, she crouched there and realized she had no way out of here except past them.

CHAPTER EIGHT

Summer heard footsteps and a scratching sound like someone had leaned against the front desk. A voice she recognized as belonging to Cameron quietly asked, "Where is she?"

She let out a deep breath. "Here."

Cameron peered behind the desk.

"What—?"

She put her finger to her lips to stop him and motioned him closer. "Look at the men."

He stood and quickly glanced at them before kneeling down in front of Summer. "They look like scientists: glasses, short hair, bad suits. They're waiting to be helped."

"Aren't they *the* men?"

He shook his head. "These men wouldn't hurt a flea."

She glared at him when she could tell he wanted to laugh. He put one hand over his mouth, turned away from her, and escaped in the direction of the stairs. Smart man.

Summer wondered if they *were* innocent men. Changing positions so that she could see over the front desk with one eye, she inspected the men. Seeing ordinary people, she stood the rest of the way. Her face hot, she said, "I'm sorry, gentlemen. I was looking for something under the desk." *Yeah, courage.* "May I help you?"

They looked at each other and shrugged. At the front desk, one of them said, "My brother and I are in town for a scientific conference. We have reservations."

Cameron sputtered, turned away from the stairs, and hurried out the front door. When he came back with a big grin on his face, Cozy had returned to the lobby. Summer sheepishly glanced in his direction. What a fool she'd made of herself.

He approached her slowly and asked, "Would you like to know what Cozy and I found?"

Summer nodded excitedly.

"Nothing."

Cozy smiled at Cameron and moved over to her usual post. Summer bit down on her annoyance.

Cameron added, "Except Cozy said all the dressers should have knickknacks and pictures on them, but one had nothing. And the strange thing is that it's room 214. The one someone ransacked. She says that once the police had told them the room could be used again, housekeeping just made the bed and put things back together. No one removed anything."

"So maybe the person who did the damage was looking for the item or items that are missing." She groaned. "Or maybe a former guest took home a souvenir and has a cheap knickknack at home on his or her mantle."

"My feelings exactly. Let's go through the clues again."

Summer sat down on the stool and ticked them off on her fingers as she went. "Don's missing. Someone trashed his quarters and room 214. His appointment book disappeared and reappeared." She looked over at Cameron to see if he still believed her on that. He seemed to be listening intently, so she continued. "We found a mysterious note in the frame of one of the pictures in his room. We found a"—she lowered her voice—"valuable, stolen, antique lamp in a guest room, and now something might be missing." She stood. "We have a lot of things that don't seem to fit together."

"Don't forget the two men who have been following you."

Summer shuddered. "I don't know how I forgot them. I haven't seen them recently. I'm not sure if I should be relieved they aren't following me or concerned because they're still there, but they're better at it. If I don't see them, how do I know which to believe?"

"If they had meant to harm you, I think they would have."

She turned to him. "That's what I thought. Maybe they're just waiting for us to lead them to something." She raised her arms in exasperation. "But what?"

"Whatever it is, I'll help you find it."

Summer watched him smile as he looked her way, and she couldn't help but smile back. "Let's search Don's office again, and when we're finished, the restaurant will be closed and we can search there." She paused after taking a few steps. "Sorry. I should have asked if you want to do more sleuthing or if you're tired."

"I'm always ready to help."

Her question from earlier that night reappeared. Was he only here because of Erin? Or was there more?

When Cameron dropped her at her condo after midnight, she trudged away from his truck. Hours going through the inn had produced nothing helpful. As her condo's door closed behind her, she decided to sleep late the next morning. A clear, well-rested head should have better ideas than an exhausted one.

~

Knock knock.

Summer shifted in the bed and pulled the pillow over her head.

Knock knock.

Blinking, she sat up, grabbed her robe, and put it on as she headed for the door. Another knock sounded on her way. Opening the door, she found her landlord waiting.

He impatiently thrust a package in her arms.

"Well—"

He spun on his heels and walked away.

The brown paper-wrapped box looked about the size of her microwave and, she thought, adjusting it in her arms, weighed about as much. After closing the door, she placed it on the floor in front of her couch.

Another knock sounded at the door and she ripped it open. "If you're here to apologize—"

The woman at the door reeled back.

"Oh, Jan, I'm sorry. I thought you were someone else."

A petite woman wearing a paint-splattered smock and a stunned expression stood outside her door. "I'm glad I'm me. I finished the painting of the inn."

Summer took the canvas from her upstairs neighbor. The inn sparkled with Christmas lights reflecting off the snow. "Jan, it's beautiful. Don will love it!"

As soon as she said it, Summer felt tears prick her eyes. When she sniffled, Jan put her hand on her arm.

"Are you okay?"

Summer nodded. "It's just been a long week."

"Do you know any more about where he could be?"

Of course her neighbor knew about her missing groom. Everyone must by now.

"Nothing more than has been in the papers."

"They'll find him. And when they do, you can get married."

Summer started to mention his other fiancée, but stopped. That hadn't been in the papers.

Jan turned and waved as she headed upstairs to her unit.

Summer didn't really have time, but she wanted to know the box's contents. Ripping off the paper, she found a wedding card tucked inside and a microwave from her Aunt Millie. A wedding present and a painting of the inn. She'd been woken for two things she didn't want or need.

The whole thing tickled her funny bone. A laugh escaped, then another. She sat down and laughed until she cried. A sob escaped as she grabbed a handful of tissues. She realized she'd stopped crying because of laughter and moved on to real crying.

Half a box of tissues later, she hiccupped and took a moment to look at her watch. Only a half hour to change and meet a client!

After hurriedly dressing and doing an extra-special makeup job to clear all evidence of "laughter," she went over to her bedroom window and pulled back a corner of the curtain. No one loitered near her car. She breathed a sigh of relief. It would be safe to drive.

Her feet felt like skipping as she walked the few steps from her car to her office, but she restrained herself and the grin that wanted to burst through at the thought. Summer Marshall, respected marketing consultant, wearing a light wool jacket and matching skirt, skipping down the sidewalk. She shouldn't feel like skipping with Don missing, but she did. When she arrived at her building, Antonio opened the door, surprising her with his presence on a Saturday.

"It is *molto bene* to see you today, *cara*."

Summer grinned. So today, Antonio was Italian. "It's always good to see you, Antonio."

He twirled his mustache, and Summer fought a laugh.

"Any news of Mr. Daily?"

Her grin fell away. "None."

"They will find him. Do not worry, *cara*." He squeezed her hand.

"I have to get ready for an appointment. Mr. Girard is coming in. You know him, don't you?"

Antonio nodded.

"I'm looking for a new marketing concept for his company. I've been so busy that I haven't come up with anything yet." Walking away, she added over her shoulder, "I'm glad you were here today."

After her appointment, she worked out some more of the preliminaries for Samantha Martin. Late in the afternoon, she raised her arms over her head to stretch and thought about taking a walk—in an open, busy, visible place—to stretch the rest of her muscles.

When the phone rang, she happily picked it up. The building felt oddly quiet on Saturdays. She was happy to have someone to talk to, and discovering that someone was Cameron was even better. "Will you be coming over to help tonight?"

He paused so long that she almost asked if he was still on the line. "I did promise my sister. I will if you need me."

She sat up straight. "No. I'll be fine."

He ended the conversation with, "Let me know if you need me."

Summer hung up the phone feeling foolish. Hadn't the two of them been working side by side in this? He'd insisted that he be included in the search. She'd become used to his presence. Well, she couldn't expect Cameron to drop everything to help her. She hadn't seen Don as her rescuer, so she didn't need to see Cameron that way.

After locking up her office for the night, Summer climbed into her car. Deciding to spend the evening at the inn, she pulled out. Maybe, by being there, she would get closer to discovering Don's whereabouts. And at least she wouldn't be home alone thinking about everything but doing nothing.

Shortly after she arrived there and pulled up a stool next to Cozy at the front desk, the door opened. Summer glanced up to smile at what she thought would be a guest and discovered Cameron standing there. Every fiber of her being danced with joy at the sight of him. She pushed that happiness down.

Cozy started talking fast when she saw Cameron. "I was about to ask this. I know Cameron is here now, but will you fill in for me for a bit? I'm hungry."

"Sure." Summer watched Cameron walk across the room toward her as Cozy raced away. "She went to get something to eat and I'm helping out. She's been at the inn every spare minute since Don's been gone, so I'm happy to do it. Make yourself comfortable, and when she comes back—" The phone rang.

A rattled groom, making reservations for his honeymoon. He said his fiancée was nearby and whispered that he wanted to know if he could pay when they arrived and still have the room guaranteed.

Feeling compelled to whisper back, she said, "No, I need a deposit now."

He said staying at the inn would be a special treat for his wife-to-be because they couldn't take a honeymoon right now. Then he asked the odd question of whether his new wife would like the room.

Summer answered, "It's beautiful. Definitely worth it."

He thanked her and told her he would call back later.

After she hung up the phone, Summer looked around and found Cameron sitting on a couch, reading a magazine. At least he hadn't felt compelled to stand at the desk and wait.

A short time later, Cozy came back, smiling. "Thanks, Summer. I needed a break."

When Summer walked over to Cameron and he didn't look up, she wondered about the compelling article he'd found. A few feet in front of him, she stopped, stunned. The magazine he was reading was upside down. "Interesting article?"

"Huh?" He set the magazine on the coffee table. "Are you ready to go in to eat?"

"Eat? Well, sure. I guess so. I hadn't really thought about dinner, but the restaurant looks fairly empty tonight. We should be served quickly."

"Oh, would you mind if I made a quick phone call? I'll meet you in there."

She'd taken a couple of steps toward the restaurant when she stopped and looked back at him. He seemed . . . edgy.

"Why don't you call from Don's office for privacy?"

Relief seemed to sweep over him. "That's a great idea."

What was going on? After taking him into Don's office,

she casually left the room. As soon as she was out of his line of sight, she ran over to the restaurant, got them a table, and ran back to listen.

Standing outside the office door, she focused intently on a vase of fresh flowers to appear nonchalant. Wanting to seem to anyone walking by that she belonged there, she pulled the flowers out of the vase and, one by one, began putting them back, carefully studying each new flower's placement. She'd only put a few of the flowers in the vase when she heard Cameron's words.

"No, I need to take it out of here. The lamp can't stay."

The flowers in her hand fell to the floor. It sounded like he planned to steal the antique lamp. No, he must be talking about some . . . other lamp. She kneeled and began picking up the flowers.

"No, I don't think I can get it out of here tonight." He sighed. "I'm planning to come back around dawn. At that hour, I should be able to get in easily and sneak the lamp out of the inn."

Summer stood and her hands closed around the flowers. No mistake. Well, at least she could save him from himself. If she kept her eyes on the lamp, he couldn't steal it.

"Goodbye." Shuffling sounds told her he'd ended the call and was heading her direction.

She quickly shoved flowers in the vase and took off running, nearly knocking over a guest on her way to the restaurant. She'd been at the table about thirty seconds when Cameron walked in.

Standing in front of her, he said, "I'm not hungry anymore. How about if we go home and get a good night's sleep?"

She blinked. "But it's only"—she looked at her watch —"six-thirty."

Visibly squirming, he said, "That's true, but we've been very busy lately and need our rest."

Summer watched him. He hadn't lied. He needed sleep so he could come back around dawn and steal the lamp. "We have been busy." She'd make sure he watched her drive away, but she would sneak back. As she started to leave, an idea occurred to her. "I'll stay here and help Cozy tonight so she can do some homework."

He started to protest but then nodded and left.

She soon heard the crunching of gravel in the parking lot as he drove away.

Summer sat at the front desk, tapping on the counter. Cozy had chosen to study on a comfortable couch. She had her feet tucked beside her and a textbook in her hand. After handling a few calls, Summer felt more and more restless. Each time she tried to focus on anything but Cameron and the lamp, her mind bounced right back to them. He couldn't really be a thief. He'd reform if he had an opportunity to think before he took the lamp. And she would give him that opportunity.

But how could she stop him? He was bigger than she was, so she couldn't tackle him and take the lamp away. The very thought was ludicrous. She couldn't call the police because she didn't want him to get in trouble. After a few minutes of thought, she decided that her best plan would be to wait for him to take it and then confront him. In fact, it was her only plan.

The lamp was safe until morning, and it was now—she looked at her watch—ten fifteen. She could go home and get a few hours of sleep. "Did that study time help, Cozy?"

Cozy stretched and smiled. "Thank you so much. If I go back to work now, I can still pass my biology test tomorrow afternoon."

When Summer stepped outside, a few lights in front of the inn were the only break in the pitch blackness of night. A block from the inn, her headlights flashed on something at the side of the road. Slowing down, she realized they were reflecting off a tail light. That tail light belonged to a truck someone had pulled off the road, one that looked exactly like Cameron's. He'd parked his truck here and left it, so he must be nearby.

Slamming on her brakes, Summer wheeled her car around. She'd bet that he had been watching, waiting for her to leave so he could make his move and sneak in. Parking in the inn's driveway so he couldn't hear her return, she sat quietly and listened and watched for a couple of minutes. Nothing moved around the inn, but that didn't mean he wasn't there.

Quietly climbing out of her car, she closed the door with a slight *thunk*. Still, nothing moved. She peered into the darkness. Where could he be hiding? He'd said he would sneak inside around dawn, so he had to be outside right now. The bushes and trees surrounding the inn were the only likely hiding places.

A plan came to mind. Fortunately, Don had given her a key to the inn's toolshed along with all the other keys. Now she just needed to find the right tool. Grateful the shed had a light inside, she searched through a multitude of tools both for groundskeeping and the inn's interior maintenance. Picking up a rake with a row of short metal tines, she thought about the job she had to do. The sharp points made it too dangerous for what she had in mind. She didn't want to hurt either of them. Putting it back, she chose a shovel.

Taking deep breaths to calm her nerves, she started around the perimeter of the lawn, poking the handle of the shovel into the bushes every few feet, but all it found were leaves. Tiptoeing along in her high heels, she hoped Cameron would think small critters caused any noise he heard. Maybe she should make a sound like a nocturnal animal.

Then she shuddered. *Ignore any thoughts about animals crawling around in the brush and climbing trees.* Looking up at the trees, she wondered if animals were watching her. An owl hooted, and she jumped. *Get a grip, Summer. You've been camping in the woods before.*

But not alone.

Then she remembered she wasn't alone tonight. Cameron hid nearby. With renewed fervor, she continued her search. When she had almost completed a circle around the inn, the shovel handle hit something.

CHAPTER NINE

"Ouch." Cameron jumped out of the bushes and rubbed his arm. "What are you trying to do?"

She threw the shovel in the bushes and whispered, "Find a thief in the dark."

"Me?" He whispered. "You're the thief. I wanted to protect you from yourself."

She whispered back, "What would I want to steal? I heard you talking to someone on the phone. I heard you say you were going to steal the lamp in the morning."

"Only so you wouldn't take it."

"That's the dumbest thing I've ever heard."

"I heard you saying you needed money, and that it was worth it."

She groaned and plunked herself down on the grass. "I hadn't planned to steal anything. I was telling a groom that he needed to pay for the room before he checked in. And the honeymoon suite is worth it."

"You're kidding?"

He sat beside her. "Nope."

"You mean I made a fool out of myself for nothing?"

"Yes." A giggle escaped her. She covered her mouth with her hand. She couldn't laugh at Cameron. A second giggle escaped. Doubling over with laughter, she gasped for breath.

"I don't see what's so—" He started laughing and put his arm around her. "This is the dumbest thing I've ever done."

Gasping for breath, she asked, "Why did you do it?"

He stopped laughing, put his hand behind her head, and pulled her toward him. "For this." His lips gently, tentatively touched hers.

She felt it down to her toes and sighed. She shouldn't be kissing him. Putting her hand on his chest to push him away, it rested on his racing heart. Did his heart beat more quickly because he was kissing her? When she slid her hands up around his neck, he groaned and leaned over her. Then he released her and moved back, and she was alone. She felt like she'd gone from the tropics to the North Pole.

He rubbed his hand over his face. "Summer, we can't do this. You're still engaged to marry someone else. You and my sister. We have to get this resolved."

She put her hands on her face and laid on the grass. "I'm so embarrassed. I'm not normally like that."

"I'm the one that started it. I apologize." He stood. "I have an idea, but it's a long shot. Why don't we both get off work early tomorrow and meet Cozy here? We can have an in-depth conversation with her and see if she knows something that can help us find Don. Something she doesn't even realize she knows."

"Great idea," she said excitedly as she stood. She started toward the inn's entrance. "But she's still here. We can talk to her tonight."

"Summer." He grabbed her arm to stop her. "You can't go

inside. You've been lying on the grass." He lifted a piece of dried grass from her hair.

The night graciously covered what she knew must be a red face. "You're right," she whispered. "How would I explain that?"

"I'll meet you here tomorrow."

His hand touched hers. Then he disappeared into the night.

Summer drove home on autopilot. When she looked in her bedroom mirror, she was thankful she hadn't passed any neighbors as she'd walked to her door. Not only were her formerly attractive clothes stained with grass and dirt, but her brown hair had grass in it. She plucked at her hair. And a leaf. Throwing her clothes in the hamper, she hurried off to take a shower. A half hour later, lying in bed, staring at the ceiling, she wondered how her life had become so complicated.

A month ago, her plans had involved marriage to a seemingly charming man. Her life had appeared to be falling into place. Now, Don had two fiancées, he had vanished, and she had spent part of her evening kissing a man she barely knew.

Don had never kissed her like that. Not even close. How could she ever look Cameron in the face again? She rolled onto her side. He had started it, though. But she had continued it. So Cameron was gorgeous, nice, and kissed like a dream. She rolled over and tried to push memories of that kiss away. A picture of him leaning toward her for the first kiss played in her mind. She rolled back onto her other side.

The bedroom windows were going to start steaming up if she didn't think about something else and, on top of that, every cell of her body cried out for sleep.

Summer's mind reeled with images of her planned wedding and everything that had happened since, including last night's kiss. She pushed those aside and indulged herself with homemade pancakes for breakfast. Pouring maple syrup over them, she purposefully shifted her mind to the office. The Girard account had been puzzling her. What was new and would create more business for the company? An idea unfolded in her mind. Writing down the details, she became more and more excited. It was perfect! Dancing around the room, she thought about Cameron. Maybe she should give him a call and share her good news.

She stopped dancing. Not only could she not call him, but she didn't know if she could ever look him in the face again. Not after the way she had been the one to turn his sweet kiss into so much more. Would he still come to the inn tonight?

Yes. He had never disappointed her.

She got ready for work, parked across the street from her office, and barreled across the busy street. She paused in the middle of the street when a horn honked. Looking up, she saw a woman in a car gesturing wildly to her. Summer smiled at her and waved.

Brakes squealed, and a car coming from the other direc tion honked. She turned and waved to it. Excitedly contin-uing across the road, she smiled to herself and enjoyed the bounce in her step. A couple of dark-haired men leaning on a car down the street looked up. Summer waved to them and walked into the building, bursting with joy.

Ann and Antonio stood by the door.

"Are you all right, *cherie*?"

She set her briefcase down. "I'm wonderful."

Ann had a panicky expression on her face. "Two cars nearly hit you."

"Nonsense, the drivers were saying good morning." She looked out across the road. "Weren't they?" Cars moved back and forth on the busy thoroughfare. Had she just walked across that road without checking for traffic?

"Were you thinking about something, *cara*?"

"I found a great solution for the Girard account!"

"I know you've wanted that account. Congratulations." Antonio smiled charmingly. "But please look before you cross any more roads."

After agreeing that she would, Summer hurried to her office and called Roger Girard. He loved the idea, so she spent most of the day finalizing her proposal for his company. Before she knew it, it was four o'clock, and she nervously stood at the front counter of the inn, waiting for Cameron to come through the door.

He stepped inside the inn and paused, looking around the room at everything but her.

Laughter bubbled inside her. He felt just as nervous as she did. From the corner of her eye, she saw Cozy watching the two of them, so she walked over and whispered to Cameron, "Let's pretend last night never happened. We have an audience."

Cameron glanced at Cozy then nodded. "Agreed. Let's get on with finding Don."

Once they found Don, she would have no reason to see

Cameron again. She would miss the part he played in her life. And after last night, she couldn't tell Don that Cameron was just a friend.

"What are the two of you doing here so early?" Cozy interrupted Summer's thoughts.

"Huh? Oh, sorry. I seem to be daydreaming a lot." She smiled and walked over to the front desk. "Probably because I haven't had much sleep."

Cozy looked from one of them to the other. "Have you had much sleep, Cameron?"

Summer saw his eyes go wide. Then he looked over at her and she stifled a groan. That was exactly what Cozy had been looking for.

Summer defused the situation by saying, "I got up early and worked at home for a while." She hid a grin with her hand when Cozy looked disappointed. "How did you do on your test?"

Cozy grinned. "Great. Thanks for giving me time to study last night."

"I'm glad it helped. Anyway, Cozy, we're here for a reason."

"Yes, we wondered if you knew something about Don's whereabouts but didn't realize the information would be helpful."

Cozy raised her hands to shoulder level. "The officer questioned me, but I couldn't think of anything useful. Don just vanished."

"He didn't give you any clues about a possible destination?"

"Oh, yes, he gave lots of clues. He was getting married, remember?"

Both Cameron and Summer rested against the front desk.

Cameron asked, "What about the honeymoon?"

"What about the honeymoon? Other than the fact that Summer should be a married woman by now and on that honeymoon."

Summer sighed. "Cozy, I have to tell you something. Something that hasn't been in the newspapers. Don had a second fiancée."

Cozy laughed. "You're kidding, of course." When they didn't agree, she said, "Aren't you kidding? Who would have two fiancées?"

"Mr. Don Daily."

Cozy sat down. "Who's the other fiancée?"

Summer pointed at him. "His sister."

"So that's why you're here?" She gave him a long glance and frowned. "Do the police know about the other fiancée?"

Cameron sighed. "We're not sure. But either way, we think the mystery is the same."

"I asked you before, Cozy, but maybe you thought you shouldn't talk about it. Do you know the location of the honeymoon? Don wouldn't tell me a thing, and it might give us a clue."

Cozy hesitated.

"You do know." Summer leaned forward. "Please tell us."

"He made me promise not to. I figured it didn't have anything to do with what had happened to him, so I didn't need to tell."

Still leaning against the counter, Summer bounced up and down. "Where were we going? Sweden? New England? He said the climate was like ours here."

Cozy grimaced. "Maybe you'd better sit down." She walked around to Summer and took her arm.

Summer refused to budge. "Why would I need to sit down to find out where I was going on my honeymoon?"

Cozy frowned. "Because he was taking you to a bed and breakfast forty-five minutes from here."

When Summer slumped against the front desk, Cozy and Cameron helped her over to a couch. Someone pressed a glass of water into her hands. For a woman who'd never fainted before her wedding day, she suddenly had a lot of people pressing glasses of water into her hands.

"Drink this," Cameron said.

The cool water helped. She opened her eyes and looked up at their concerned faces. "I'm fine," she squeaked. She took a deep breath and then another. Feeling more herself, she said, "What I don't understand is why he wouldn't tell me." She stood and paced across the room. "I bought clothes for a honeymoon. Beautiful clothes." She stopped and looked at them. "All I needed were jeans."

Cozy looked concerned. "I'm sure you'll be able to wear the clothes somewhere else. You didn't waste the money."

Summer sat down on the nearest couch. "This isn't about the money." She stared blankly out the windows and sighed. Turning toward Cameron, she said, "Let's go see if the place can give us any clues."

Cameron looked at her suspiciously. "Are you sure you want to do this? You don't look yourself."

"I'm fine."

Cozy wrote down the name and address of the inn. Then she carefully walked beside Summer to the parking lot, looking prepared to catch her if needed. "Come back and tell me if you find out anything."

Summer stood beside the truck, tapping on the window.

She managed a nod of agreement toward Cozy who then went back inside.

As Cameron put the key in his truck door, a loud noise rang out. Glancing around, she couldn't find its source. The noise sounded again.

"Someone's shooting at us! Get down!" He dropped to the ground, and she did the same. "Lay as still as you can. They can't hit something they can't see."

She turned her head slightly to get a better look at the parking lot. Not even a leaf stirred. When everything remained quiet, Summer started to stand. "I don't think it was a shot. It must have been a car backfiring." Halfway to her feet, a third boom sounded. She screamed and fell to the ground.

"Summer? Are you all right?" Cameron scooted along the ground to her.

Face down, she pressed herself to his side. She grabbed a hold of his hand and squeezed it tightly before speaking. "Mmph."

"What?"

She lifted her head off the ground and said, "I'm fine."

"Let's crawl over to the inn's door. Agreed?"

She murmured agreement and felt him start to move to safety. They inched along the ground as a child would to play a game, but this was no game. Her arms were aching by the time she banged her head against the door.

"It opens out, so we can't push it open and slip inside. I'm going to stand and open the door."

She squeezed his hand. "Be careful."

Sounds of laughter came from inside the inn.

Cameron looked puzzled. "No one laughs when they're being shot at."

Summer agreed. "So what's going on?" Another blast rang out. Summer pressed herself to the ground. Then, seconds later, a laugh she recognized as Cozy's came from inside the inn.

Cameron stood.

She tugged on his pant leg. "Are you crazy?"

"Summer, this can't be gunshots." He pointed toward the inn. *"They're laughing."*

Summer glanced around before slowly rising to her feet.

When they entered through the door, two boys who she guessed were about ten years old stood in front of Cozy, who was holding onto several firecrackers, talking sternly and shaking her finger at them. Then she started laughing. "I know I should be mad and tell the police about you"—the boys looked scared at this—"but then they'd know I hid under my desk."

Summer whispered to Cameron, "Don't say anything. I feel like a fool."

"You and me both. I won't say a word."

Cozy looked up. "I thought you'd left. It sounded like someone had fired a gun at the inn, but it was just these two shooting off firecrackers behind it." She giggled. Then she seemed to change characters and glared at the boys sternly. "But they won't do it again, will they?"

The two of them solemnly shook their heads.

Summer could see that Cozy had this under control. "We're going now." She went out the door with Cameron close behind.

When they were halfway to his truck, a police car came around the corner with its siren blaring. The tires ground to a stop. An officer opened the door, pulled out a gun, and pointed it at them. "Freeze!"

Summer raised her hands in true criminal style. She jabbed Cameron in his side with her elbow, and he raised his.

"We've had a report of gunshots."

Summer started to lower her hands. "That wasn't—"

"Don't move!"

"Kids shooting fireworks," Summer stammered and gestured toward the inn.

The officer lowered his gun. "Fireworks?"

"Yes." Summer kept her hands raised, just in case.

He holstered his gun. "Lower your hands. Is there anyone who can verify this?"

"The woman at the front desk. The two boys who shot the firecrackers were with her a few minutes ago."

When they stepped inside, a young couple came down the stairs with their wheeled luggage thumping on each step. With uncombed hair and clothes askew, they had a look of desperation. Before they reached the bottom of the stairs, the man said, "We want to check out of here."

Cozy answered, "But I let you know the noise was just boys with fireworks."

"Criminals ransacking rooms, a missing groom . . . We thought it would be okay, but we want out, and we want our money back. Now."

Summer, Cameron, and the officer watched from where they stood near the door while Cozy helped the couple. Then the man and woman practically ran out the door with the wheels of the luggage barely touching the ground.

Emilie raced around the corner with a feather duster in her hand, yelling "Shots! Shots!" and ran straight into the officer. Bouncing off him, she landed on her bottom on the floor. When she looked up and saw who she'd run into, she made a startled jump backward. Tucking her gray hair into her bun, she stared at the officer without speaking.

Cameron held out his hand to help her up. As Emilie grabbed it, the officer took hold of her other arm, and they pulled her to her feet.

Summer sank onto one of the couches and leaned back. "Emilie, it was fireworks."

"I see." Emilie retied her apron around her ample waist.

"Are you all right, miss?" the officer asked the housekeeper.

"Yes." Then, just as someone might tuck a pencil behind their ear, Emilie tucked the feather duster there.

Summer eyes opened wide at the sight.

The housekeeper said, "If it's okay with you, I will return to work." Emilie twisted a ring on her finger. She seemed nervous.

Summer looked over at the officer as he nodded and answered, "Thank you. We'll call if we need anything else."

The woman bustled out of the room, feathers flopping with each step.

The officer closed his notebook and then, with an astounded tone in his voice, said, "I wouldn't have guessed a feather duster could be put there." Clearing his throat, he resumed his serious demeanor, "Any news on your fiancé?"

"No, I haven't heard from him since the wedding day."

He looked from her to Cameron and raised his eyebrows. "Please let us know if he contacts you."

She nodded. After the inn's front door closed behind the officer, Cameron hurried over to the window.

"Cameron, the officer gave us a look that said he suspected we had knocked off Don."

She heard a vehicle start up and then the crunching sound of tires on gravel as it drove away.

"He's leaving." Cameron turned back. "You're right about how he looked at us. Summer, we know where Don might be. We have a clue, and we should have told the police officer about it."

"It's only an idea about where he might be. Let's see if we discover anything. Besides, I'd like a moment alone with Don if he's there."

As they drove out of the city toward her former honeymoon destination, Summer rolled down the window on Cameron's truck and felt the wind blow on her face. They might be on their way to Don. So why didn't she feel happy? Glancing over at Cameron, she noticed him tapping on the steering wheel in a steady staccato. Clearly stressed out, he flexed his shoulders and frowned.

Then it all became clear to her. If Don was at the bed and breakfast, he had probably just run away from the wedding, but he'd left her concerned about him and spending time trying to help him. Never mind the fact that she'd originally just wanted to tell him she couldn't marry him. Summer tapped on the windowsill and pondered the situation. Out of the corner of her eye, she saw Cameron glance over from behind the wheel.

"Anything wrong?"

"Nope."

"Are you sure?"

"Yep." They pulled into the bed and breakfast's parking lot a minute later. She wordlessly stepped out of the truck, slammed the door, and started for the open front door. The owner greeted them and confirmed that not only had Don registered there, but he was in his room. Fortunately, he must have covered his single occupancy of the room origi-nally booked for two by saying his fiancée would be joining him later. The woman gave Cameron a questioning glance but sent them right up.

Standing in front of Don's door, she paused and took a deep breath. Her fiancé was inside. The man who had promised to marry her. And Erin.

She pounded on his door.

$\mathcal{A}$ handsome, fair-haired man answered the door. Her groom. No man had ever looked more stunned.

"Summer!" He blinked his eyes and stood back. "It's . . . good to see you."

She walked through the door, followed by Cameron.

"What's he doing here?" Don moved to bar his entrance.

"Let Cameron in." She walked over and sat on a chair, trying for a calm appearance. She wouldn't let Don see how distressed he'd made her. Looking up at him, she said, "So, I guess you know the police have been searching for you." She glanced over at Cameron, who hovered near the open door.

"The police? Why? I didn't do anything."

She glared at him.

"Well, nothing that's a crime."

"Two wives? That's bigamy!" Cameron shouted.

"I don't have two wives. I had two fiancées. That isn't illegal. I hadn't planned to marry both of them." He sat down on the end of the bed. "I'm sorry, Summer, but I needed time to think." He looked at Cameron. "Does he have to be here?"

Summer nodded. "He's Erin's brother, and he's been a good friend through all of this. He stays."

"All of what? A couple of weeks ago, I didn't come to my wedding."

Cameron made a gruff noise. Summer glared at him and he looked back sheepishly.

"You vanished eleven days ago and, since then, your quarters at the inn and a guest room were ransacked, a mysterious note was discovered, and"—she stood—"a valuable stolen lamp was found in one of the guest rooms."

Don gasped. Glaring at her, he folded his arms over his chest. "I don't believe it. You're making it up."

"To what end?" Cameron ambled over to Don with an expression that said smoke could be coming out his ears soon.

Don ignored Cameron. Turning to her, he said, "Summer, I would really like to talk to you. I've done a lot of thinking and I want to apologize to you." He glanced back at Cameron. "Alone."

She sighed. "Would you mind leaving us for a few minutes, Cameron? I'll meet you downstairs."

Cameron hesitated, but she pleaded with her eyes, and he left. He had been supportive, but she needed to do this alone.

When the door closed, she looked back at Don. "What did you want to say to me?" She sat back down and tried for a relaxed appearance.

Don stared at her. "You don't seem the same, Summer."

"I'm the same. If I seem emotional, it's probably because you left me concerned about you, thinking you needed help. But you were just a snake that slithered away from the wedding. Make that *weddings*."

He winced. "I can see you're mad at me. Let me explain."

"I'm listening." She blew on her fingertips, then brushed them on her shirt.

He walked across the room. "I got cold feet."

"From what I understand, that happens to a lot of grooms, but not many of them disappear from sight." She glared at him. "And elude the police."

He sat down on the end of the bed. "Again, I ask, what do the police have to do with me?"

"You were missing, and someone had trashed your quarters. Your beloved fiancée and your loyal employees at the inn thought something had happened to you."

"Sarcasm doesn't suit you, Summer." He studied her.

She stared back. He really was handsome. Standing at about six feet tall, with perfect, sculpted features, he appeared to have stepped from the pages of a magazine. His hair was a natural, bleached shade of blond that made him look like he'd just put his surfboard away after hours on the beach. But Don had never picked up a surfboard, and he wasn't a beach bum. He had exceptional manners. Even now.

He stepped forward and kneeled beside her chair. "I want to apologize for the problems I've obviously caused you."

She looked at him. Down on his knees, he seemed serious, but he had seemed serious the whole time she had known him. Including the day before he'd left her at the altar.

"Please, get up and tell me what happened the day of the wedding."

He hesitantly looked up at her. Standing, he said, "I put on my tux and looked in the mirror." He glanced over at a mirror on the wall as though remembering. "I looked great, but I couldn't figure out which woman should be my wife. All I could think of were the years ahead of me. Marriage seemed so . . . permanent. Still, I went over to the church for our wedding and parked the car. I pictured marrying you. Then I went over to the church where Erin waited, and I thought about her. I realized I wasn't ready to be married, so I picked up my suitcases from the inn and ran. I'd already paid for this room."

"So the thought of being married seemed unpleasant to you. Even though you had a choice of potential brides?"

"Yes. No! It wasn't you. It wasn't her. I was afraid to get married."

"And what about the wonderful honeymoon that you had planned for us?" She motioned to the surrounding room. "This is a short drive from the inn."

He sat on the bed looking dejected. "I'm sorry. This seemed like an acceptable place for a honeymoon."

She guiltily looked around the room. This B and B would be a charming destination.

Don smiled at her. "I've had time to think about marriage. I pictured all the enjoyable evenings we had while we worked on projects for the inn."

She winced. How could she have considered marrying a man she never had fun with?

"And remember when we went out to eat?"

She relaxed. They *had* enjoyed dinners at Mama Maria's. "Yes, that was pleasant."

"How are things at the inn?"

She blinked. "Huh?"

"I asked how things were at the inn."

"Things at the inn are . . . fine." Summer stood and smoothed her skirt. "Do you have anything else to say, or can I leave now?"

"I see you're still wearing your ring."

She looked at her left hand. Had he always changed subjects like this? "That's because I'm engaged." She looked over at him. "Until now." She moved to take off the ring.

He hurried over, kneeled before her, and covered her hand with his, preventing her from sliding it off her finger.

She tried to shake loose of his hold. "What are you doing?"

"I want to marry you."

She leaned back in the chair, grateful for its presence. "What?" she whispered.

He looked into her eyes. "I said, I want to marry you."

"You must be kidding?" She searched his eyes for a clue to his sincerity. Regaining her composure, she sat straight and tried to shake her hand loose again. She didn't have the heart to tell him she'd planned to call off the wedding anyway. What if she'd also had cold feet earlier and really wanted to marry him? Confusion swirled around her. "I've been through a lot in the past week and a half. I'll have to think about this."

He moved closer. "Please, Summer. We're good together. Remember us sitting at the inn, talking about the business, working on the paperwork. Wasn't that nice? Think about the night your favorite client introduced us."

She stopped trying to get away and pictured her and Don at the inn. It was a pleasant picture. Marriage to Don had always seemed . . . pleasant. Everything about being with Don was pleasant. But never exciting or joyful. Her client did see Don as a son. Even so, while he generally had good judgment, that wasn't a recommendation for marriage. An image of her and Don running the inn came to mind. Also pleasant.

Then she remembered. She knew something now that she hadn't known then. "What about your other fiancée?"

"I want to marry *you*."

Summer shook her head to clear it. She'd wanted to walk away from the wedding eleven days ago. But she must have wanted to marry Don when he'd asked her or she wouldn't have said "yes." Maybe it would simply take a while to get used to the idea again.

"You *promised* to marry me, Summer."

She *had* promised to marry him. Did she still want to? The days since the wedding crashed in on her. "You also promised to marry Erin."

Don's gaze locked with hers. "I will spend the rest of my life apologizing for that if I need to."

He seemed sincere, but hadn't he always seemed to be genuine? "How can I trust that it won't happen again?"

"It wasn't the same as with you. Erin and I spent time together when she was planning an event for work. I said one thing that escalated, and before I knew it, we were engaged."

"That must be the most ridiculous thing I've ever heard."

Not one to give up when there was something he wanted, he tried one more time. "Marry me, Summer. We'll have a great life."

The past, present, and possible futures were too much to consider right now. Standing, she said, "I'm not sure, Don. Let me think about it."

He leaned back on his heels with a stunned expression. Obviously, the possibility that she wouldn't agree with him hadn't entered his mind. Summer would have laughed at the expression on his face under other circumstances.

"When will you know?"

"By tomorrow." Summer looked around for his suitcases. "Let's get you packed so you can go back to the inn."

He hesitated. "I thought I should stay here. Since all these things are happening."

Her eyes opened wide. "You aren't coming back? At least the police will be glad to know you aren't hurt."

"Actually, Summer, I also thought it would be better to leave things as they are. The mystery should be solved soon, right?"

She nodded. "I hope so. But why don't you want to come back?"

"It just seems foolhardy to get involved in all this."

She contemplated his reasoning. "I guess that makes sense."

"By the way, what happened to Erin?"

"She went on the honeymoon with her mother."

He nodded as though he was thinking about something. It occurred to her that he might be thinking of proposing to Erin too. But he sounded sincere when he offered, "You can call me if you need my help."

At the door, he kissed her so quickly it felt like a breeze over her lips. When she pulled him closer, he stepped back with a stunned expression on his face. Kissing Don didn't feel anything like kissing Cameron.

Cameron waited at the inn's front door. She pasted on a smile when she saw him.

"Are you all right, Summer?"

She nodded and continued fake-smiling.

He put his hands on her shoulders and looked into her eyes. "Are you sure?"

"I'm fine." She stepped back from him. "Don asked me to marry him."

He stared at her, then back to the bed and breakfast. "You're marrying *him*?" He pointed up at Don's window.

"I told him I'd think about it." She walked up to his truck. "No matter what, though, you and I can solve this mystery."

He looked up at Don's window again. "Where's Mr. Daily?"

"He isn't coming."

"He . . . isn't coming?"

"Nope." She opened the truck's door. "I want to thank you, Cameron, for being such a good friend to me."

Summer woke with something poking her in the back. Moving around didn't help. Opening her eyes, she blinked to clear her vision and realized she'd fallen asleep on her couch. She reached around to her back and found one of the couch's decorative buttons digging into it. The last thing she remembered was coming home and sitting on the couch.

Cameron had been so angry with Don and with her confusion about him that she'd asked if she would see him again.

He'd replied, "I told you I'd help you and I will. I've always been here when you needed me."

What an odd thing to say, she'd thought as he squealed his tires pulling out of the inn's parking lot. She'd gone inside to tell Cozy that they'd found Don safely tucked into the B and B. Then, not understanding Cameron's obvious anger, she'd gone home and tried to figure out the situation. That was the last thing she remembered.

Sitting up, she groaned when her stiff muscles protested. Early morning rays of sun told her she'd spent the whole night here. A glance at the clock confirmed it. Five thirty.

Her mind turned to Don and his proposal. She could be married next week. He had many good qualities.

She closed her eyes and tried to count them. He was loyal. She shook her head. Was a man with two fiancées loyal? She didn't think so. He was kind. She shook her head again. Not only had he run out on their wedding, but he'd refused to leave his sanctuary to help solve the mystery. They had spent many companionable hours together at the inn. She nodded. Yes, they got along well together. But you could describe a relationship with a dog or cat the same way. He was handsome. Character was far more important than appearance, though.

She pictured the times they'd kissed. No sparks had skyrocketed through the air.

After a long, hot shower, she pulled back the curtain on her bedroom window to see if anyone hovered near her car. No watchers. On the way to her vehicle, she stopped. Yesterday morning came flooding back. Two men. She'd waved at two men as she crossed the street. Summer put her hands to her mouth. She'd almost been hit by a car and waved to her watchers. She needed to concentrate on what she was doing.

Running, she got to her car in seconds and raced to the safety of her office. A frustrating day there had left her in a somewhat grumpy mood, and the off-and-on rain hadn't helped. She had hoped that a new client she'd been pursuing would call her office today, but he hadn't. Thankfully, Antonio never failed to amuse her. When she'd walked by him after lunch, a man with a French accent had asked him a question, and Antonio had replied in what sounded like beautiful French.

Thankfully, the day had passed quickly, and she arrived at

the inn before dark. Now that she knew Don was safe, she needed to get back in the routine of doing paperwork for the inn.

She plodded through the lobby, went straight to Don's office, and plopped down in his desk chair. Instead of working, she leaned forward and rested her head on the desk. With everything that had been going on in her life, she needed a moment to think.

"Are you all right, Summer?"

She jumped. Cozy watched her from the doorway. Forcing a bright smile, she said, "I'm fine. Why do you ask?"

Cozy gave a tentative smile. "Because you're the most industrious person I know. I've never seen you doing nothing." She sat in one of the chairs in front of Don's desk.

Summer's smile wavered. "It must be the mystery that has me behaving this way."

Cozy stood. "Sure, the mystery. By the way, you don't have to do this anymore." She pointed at the pile of papers on the desk.

Summer stared at the desk. "You're right. Don didn't pay me. I did this for love." She looked up at Cozy. "But he proposed again."

"Really?" Cozy stepped closer to the desk. "Are you considering the proposal?"

Summer sighed. "I'm not sure."

Cozy fell into a chair. "This is amazing. You've got Cameron."

"I don't have Cameron."

"You could."

"He's my friend."

Cozy grinned. "Great!"

Summer laughed. "Now that you know about his sister, I can tell you that's the only reason he's been helping me."

"Are you sure?" The phone rang, so Cozy reached over and answered it. Handing it to Summer, she mouthed, "Mr. Daily."

Summer listened to Don and waved to Cozy when the other woman left the office. Searching through the paperwork on his desk, she found what he'd described. "Yes, I found it. I'll take care of it this time, but you know you'll need to hire someone to take over what I've been doing."

Cameron walked in with a small backpack and sat down in a chair. He didn't look his usual happy self. In fact, he almost looked sad.

"Don, it would be ridiculous for me to work for you for free if I don't marry you. Even if we do get married, we should have some time to relax." There was a pause. "Don . . . Don—" Summer hung up the phone.

Cameron smiled, but it looked forced. Then he walked over and put his hand on her shoulder. "How are things?"

As he touched her, the usual warmth moved from his hand through her body. Feeling like she'd plugged into an electric blanket, she pushed back her chair and worked to find her voice. "Do you have any new ideas about the mystery?"

He gave her the first natural smile she'd seen since he entered the room. "I had a brilliant idea. I checked out some books on cryptology and private investigations."

Relaxing, she smiled back. "That *is* a brilliant idea."

He poured the contents of the backpack on the desk. "Which do you want to start with?"

She studied the books. "Why don't we work on the note?

That was the first clue." She frowned. "Or was it a clue? We don't know how long that note sat in the frame."

"Are you sure you have no idea? Do you know when the room was last painted?"

Summer nodded. "It was painted in June. And, at the time, I didn't think the pictures were matted well, so they went to an art shop to be redone." Nodding, she said, "The note is new."

"So we'll begin with the first clue and cryptology." Smiling, he handed her one of the books. "Do you have your copy of the note? I have mine here."

She found the photocopy in her purse. With a book in hand, she settled back to read. Cameron plucked a notebook out of a zippered pocket on the pack—he certainly came prepared—and seemed to make notes as he read his book. An hour later, Summer threw hers on the desk. "I can barely understand the different codes they're talking about, let alone figure out our note. How about you?"

He scratched out the last thing he'd written and shook his head. "Let's trade books. Maybe then something will catch our attention."

Summer opened his book and glanced over the first page. Glaring at Cameron, she said, "Have you noticed anything different about the book you're holding?"

Sheepishly, Cameron looked up. "This one appears to be a cryptology manual for experts."

"And I thought my mind wasn't working well. The one you were using should be subtitled 'Cryptology for Beginners.'"

"Think so? Then you should find something helpful in there." Cameron intensely studied the book in his hands. A while later, he set it on the desk and picked up the third volume on the subject. She smiled to herself. He'd found the book as impossible as she had.

This book's approach made decoding seem simple. She pulled out some scratch paper and tried the various methods on their note, but it didn't seem to fit any of the codes.

Cameron scribbled away again. When he stopped writing, he wadded up the paper and threw it in the trash. "This is impossible. It almost seems to be a foreign language."

She looked at the note. "You know, you're right. The words are rhythmic, not nonsensical. Like a language."

"Then I have an idea." Cameron set his book on Don's desk. "I know the head of the foreign language department at the university. I'll ask her to look at it, and we can meet her tomorrow afternoon."

Summer glanced at her watch. "Wow. It's eleven o'clock. The other books could have valuable information in them, so let's each take a book home and, if we have time, we can look it over."

Cameron stood and put one of the books on private investigation in his pack. "Can we leave these here?"

She chose a book for herself before stacking the rest in the bookcase in the corner of the room.

He laughed, but it didn't sound genuine. "I guess we can. Don won't need his office anytime soon."

Summer felt like she should stick up for Don. She was considering marrying him, wasn't she? "He feels it would be best if he stayed away until the mystery is solved."

"I'm sure that is wisest. For him." He went out the door before she could comment.

She grabbed her purse and headed for her car. Cameron seemed to enjoy taunting her about Don.

Angrily walking into her apartment a short time later,

Summer started to slam the door, then caught herself. Her neighbors didn't deserve that. Sighing, she gently closed the door to her home, the one she'd thought would soon be on the market. For months, she had thought of the inn as her future home. It had seemed warm and comfortable before, but now it seemed more a place of business and less a home. She was glad she'd planned to wait until after the honeymoon to sell her condo.

After church the next morning, she went to the inn, glad to move inside again and away from the grim, cloudy weather that threatened to depress her. The inn's gardener passed her as she walked toward the front desk. The normally placid man grumbled something and left through the door.

"What's with him?" she asked Cozy.

"Someone took his favorite shovel. Seems he can't do his work properly without *that* shovel." The phone rang, and she reached for it.

Embarrassed, Summer looked up at the ceiling. She knew more or less where to find the shovel. "I'm going for a short walk," she whispered, and Cozy nodded while confirming a phone reservation.

Summer stopped at the line of bushes that edged the parking lot. In the daylight, the vegetation was more dense than she remembered. Maybe she could buy the gardener a new shovel and sneak it into the shed. No. She shook her head. If he wanted a new one, he would have already bought one. Don might be conservative with his money, but he knew the grounds had to look good.

Maybe it would be easy to get through the bushes. Holding a waist-high bush aside to make an entrance for herself, she took a step into them. When she let go, the bush snapped around her like a living tutu. Pushing her way through for a few feet, she stopped. She couldn't even see the ground, let alone a shovel.

This wasn't working. The shovel was hiding under a bush, so she needed to look under bushes. Crouching, she waddled around the bushes like a duck. She waddled by so many neatly groomed bushes that she lost count. Then a patch of slippery, damp weeds that the gardener had missed caught her off guard.

"Whoa!" she called as she scrambled to stay upright. Her elbows hit the ground and spared the rest of her. When she forced her way upright, she backed into a tree. Looking back at the tree, she groaned. A pine tree oozing sap. The beautiful —well, formerly beautiful—pale-green pantsuit she wore now had grass stains and pine sap on it. Plus—she brushed at her chest—dirt and dried grass stuck to it. She ducked down and continued her search.

"Summer," a male voice called from far off.

"What?" she yelled back.

"Where are you?"

She recognized Cameron's voice now, and he sounded only a few feet away. "I'm under a bush." She waddled a few more feet.

"May I ask why?"

Speaking with a hushed voice, she said, "I'm looking for the shovel I threw into the woods the other night. It seems to be the gardener's favorite, and he wants it." She grinned. Then embarrassment took over. The shovel reminded her of the kiss they'd shared. Looking around, she spotted the shovel a few feet away. "I see it!" Stretching toward the handle, she grabbed it and tried to stand. Nothing happened.

"Help!" she said so only he could hear her. "I'm caught on something."

He reached down through the bushes, pulled her out still clutching the shovel, and then set her on some grass. He certainly had a lot of upper body strength. What would it feel like to have those muscled arms around her? *Forget that thought, Summer.*

He put one hand on each of her shoulders and studied her, smiling. "You're covered with nature."

"At least I found the shovel." She held it up and grinned.

"Right. The shovel." He first looked at the garden tool in her hand, then to her. Staring into her eyes, he gently massaged her shoulders. His gaze shifted to her lips, and her heart picked up speed.

Summer felt her mouth go dry. When she licked her lips, he groaned and pulled her closer.

"Summer!" Cozy called from the direction of the inn. "Phone call, Summer!"

Summer shouted, "I'll be there in a minute."

Cameron jumped and rubbed his ears. "Ouch."

"I guess I should have stepped away before yelling, huh?" Her lips twitched as she fought laughter.

Cameron rolled his eyes.

When Summer started to walk away, he grabbed her and gave her a quick kiss on the lips. She dropped the shovel and reached for him.

"Summer!" Cozy shouted.

This time, she sounded nearby. The other woman would be here any second, and she didn't want to see anyone until she'd cleaned up. Stumbling away, Summer thought of Don. An image of him kneeling in front of her, proposing, came into her mind. The two men were very different.

When she passed the inn's windows, she caught her reflection and cringed. Slowly opening the inn's front door, she peered around it into the lobby. All clear. Cozy must still be out searching for her, and the door to Don's quarters should be open.

Inside his rooms, she stared at a mirror in horror. Her knotted hair had bits of brush in it, and she'd probably ruined her suit jacket. Could a dry cleaner remove pine sap? She didn't think so. After brushing her hair, she took off her jacket and threw it over a chair. A second look at Don's mirror revealed a much improved Summer. When she stepped out of Don's quarters, she ran into Cozy.

"I wondered where you'd gone. Don insisted on holding while I found you, and he hasn't been patient about it. Got to go. Someone's checking out."

Summer entered Don's office and picked up the phone. Don had gone from impatient to livid.

"Where have you been?" he demanded.

"In the woods. Did you need something?"

"I thought of something else you need to take care of. It's important."

"I have a piece of paper ready; go ahead."

He outlined the business matter, and then hung up. His behavior would have been unacceptable for a boss. From a man who wanted to marry her, it was shocking. The phone was still in her hand when Cameron walked in a few minutes later.

"Is someone on the phone?"

Setting it down, she looked up at Cameron.

"Cozy said Don called."

She nodded. "I have one thing to do for him."

"You know, you don't have to do these things."

"Cozy said that, and I told Don the same thing. It's just easier to do it right now and not leave it for someone else." She looked around the room and wistfully added, "I always liked it here."

Cameron scowled. "The language professor I mentioned came through for us. Here."

"*Salmon, eggs, milk, butter, bread.* What does this mean?"

"It looks like a grocery list. Someone deliberately sent us in a false direction. The note seems to mean absolutely nothing." He walked over to a chair and plopped down in it.

"What language is it?"

"Norwegian with the first letter of each word moved to the end. The professor likened it to Norwegian Pig Latin."

She leaned forward, her head in her hands. "I can't think of anyone I know who speaks Norwegian. Maybe there is no mystery." She leaped to her feet and lunged for the phone so quickly that Cameron shrank back in his chair.

She smiled as she spoke into the phone. "Mr. Daily, please." Every time she mentioned Don, he grimaced. He needed to let go of what had happened with the weddings. She had, and the situation had impacted her life more than his. "Don, what do you know about a Tiffany-style lamp in guest room 221?"

Don impatiently answered that a lamp was a lamp and that he'd probably bought it at a flea market. Then he curtly asked if that was why she'd called.

"Yes, that's all," she said while smiling for Cameron's benefit. She'd never noticed that Don didn't like being bothered with details. An inn had a lot of details to handle and, without realizing it, she'd taken over many of them. She sat down in her chair, satisfied with his answer. "I'm right. There is no mystery."

Cameron leaned forward. "And how did you once again come to this brilliant conclusion?"

"I asked Don about the lamp. He said a lamp is a lamp to him, so he probably bought it thinking it was just lighting and nothing special." She paused. "Of course, that doesn't explain who trashed Don's quarters." She flung her arms out at her sides.

"Or why someone would alter a grocery list, then put it in a picture frame?"

She thought about her two pursuers and shuddered. "I keep wanting this mystery to be nothing. But it exists, and we have to solve it, don't we?"

"Yes, there is a mystery." He sighed. "But I'm willing to let the police solve it. I think we should call them tonight and tell them about the lamp if we don't discover anything new in the next couple of hours."

Summer nodded agreement. Then, walking beside him into the lobby, she said, "We need some fresh, new ideas about this mystery. Maybe—"

Cozy rushed over and interrupted the conversation. "I have a brilliant idea. In fact, I wish I'd thought of it sooner. It might be easier for you two to figure things out if you stay here."

Summer turned to Cameron. "It makes sense. We might find inspiration here. But in the morning, we have to drive to our own offices. I may need more tea to get going."

"I don't mind if it means we can solve this mystery sooner. We would get a much better feel for things if we were here."

Summer looked away. He wanted to fulfill his promise to help. Then he would get away from her as quickly as he could. Maybe that would be best.

"I hoped you'd like the idea." Cozy handed a room key to each of them. "We provide robes, shampoo, and other toiletries." She walked back to the front desk and reached under it. "Other than these, you should have everything you need." Two new toothbrushes were in her hand.

Cameron laughed and took the toothbrushes from her, handing one to Summer and putting one in his coat pocket. "You're very good at your job."

She leaned on the counter. "Tell that to the boss when he comes back. Maybe I'll get a raise."

Cameron climbed the stairs in front of Summer. When they arrived at the top, she asked, "Which room did Cozy give you?" He held out the key, and she pointed left. "You're that way. And I'm in one of the honeymoon suites. Cozy knows it's my favorite room." She walked over and put the key in the lock. "I'll meet you in an hour for dinner."

"It looked busy just now. Are you sure we can get a table tonight?"

"There's a table waiting for Don and me. It's one of the perks of being the boss's fiancée." She laughed self-consciously when she realized what she'd said.

After an uneventful but never-boring-with-Cameron dinner, she tucked herself into bed early, wearing a T-shirt with the inn's logo on it as a nightgown. As she fluffed her pillow and relaxed into it, Summer remembered they'd planned to call the police tonight. Yawning widely, she snuggled into the covers. She'd get up and go knock on his door in a few minutes.

The next time she looked at the clock, it was just after nine. She could hear something in her room . . . moving. A rodent? A chair scooted across the floor. *A very large rodent or a person.* She hoped for the rodent. Heart beating wildly, she offered a silent prayer.

"It's only me."

Summer turned on the lamp. Cameron stood next to her

bed wearing the clothes he'd had on yesterday. His hair stood up in odd places and his clothes looked rumpled, but he looked good. He always looked good. "Why are you in my room?" Pulling the blankets more tightly around herself, her heart continued to race, but she honestly wasn't sure if it was due to danger or because Cameron was nearby.

He threw her clothes at her. "Get out of bed and get dressed. We have to leave. Now."

She spun her finger in a circle. "Turn your back." He sighed but turned around. She pulled off her makeshift nightgown and replaced it with her bra and blouse before climbing out of bed. After putting on her suit trousers, she slipped into her shoes and asked, "Where are we going?"

"Hurry, Summer. We've only got a couple of minutes."

"I'm ready."

He pulled her out the door and down the stairs.

"What's going on?"

"We're about to be arrested."

"What?" she yelled and dug in her heels to stop. "What are you talking about? We haven't done anything."

He tugged her, and she moved with him again through the lobby and out the door. After opening the passenger door to his truck, he lifted her inside and pushed the lock before slamming it shut. Had he gone insane? Had the last couple of weeks been more than he could take? She struggled to open the door, but Cameron climbed in and backed out before she could. When he put his hand on her arm, she jumped.

"Relax, Summer. I'm only going to drive far enough away that we'll have time to figure out what to do. I don't want to be in separate cells tonight."

She fought to stay calm. "Please tell me what's going on."

"A judge stayed in room 214 about a month ago for an anniversary celebration. His wife fancied a miniature framed portrait that sat on their dresser so much that the judge asked if he could buy it. Don sold it to him. A friend who dabbles in antiques came to his house for dinner. The friend thought the painting appeared hundreds of years old and valuable. The couple asked Frank about it tonight. Not only was it genuine, but it was stolen. The judge called the police in front of Frank. Good friend that he is, Frank called me as soon as they left. He estimated that we had five minutes to get out ahead of the police."

"We just need to explain the situation to police. We don't have to run. The inn is Don's, not ours."

"He's missing, remember? We've been here almost every time they came."

She groaned. "You're right. Next question: Why would Frank call you?"

"Self-preservation. He'd visited the inn recently, so he thought he might get implicated in the crime if we weren't able to solve the mystery before we were questioned."

When they were a minute up the road, Cameron pointed to the rearview mirror. "We got out just in time."

Summer turned around and watched three cars with flashing lights pull into the inn. She breathed a sigh of relief and turned back. "We had agreed to call the police tonight, but we both forgot. We'd probably be fine now if we had." She touched his arm. "If we don't figure this out by tomorrow morning, we had better turn ourselves in."

"Agreed. I felt that if we could spend a couple of hours talking, considering all the new evidence, we might be able to solve this. But I can't think of any place to go where they won't find us."

Summer looked up at the sign they were approaching. "Drive away from the city." Cameron remained silent as the miles ticked off. Almost an hour later, she had him take an exit off the interstate, then another turn. They drove for a short time more. "Go right."

Cameron wheeled the truck onto a side road. "Where are we going?"

"A place I know. Turn left."

He turned the truck onto the road, and gravel flew. "How far do I go before I turn again? I'd like more than a second's notice this time."

She squinted, trying to see past the light of the headlights. "Pull in here."

He whipped into the turnout and switched off the engine. "Thanks for the notice. I appreciated it."

"Sorry." She turned up her hands. "I've only been here in the daylight."

Looking out the window, he asked, "Where are we? I can only see tall trees illuminated by the moon."

"We're at my favorite place to relax. A friend's parents own the land and have a weekend cabin up the road. I come here when I need to think, and I know we need to do that right now." She pointed toward the woods. "A short distance in, there's a beautiful spot next to a little stream where we can hide and work on the mystery."

"We could just sit here." A car came around the corner. When its headlights shined into the cab of the truck, he pushed her down. "On second thought . . ." Reaching under his seat, he took out a flashlight. After turning it on, he opened his door and stepped down onto the gravel.

She scooted over the seat and climbed out on his side of the truck since the trees were so close on hers. She took a deep breath. The air smelled so clean and fresh. Their hike would have been wonderful—if they hadn't been running from the law.

Cameron went to the back of his truck. "I went camping with Luke right before the . . ." He looked at her. "A couple of weeks ago. I haven't had a chance to unpack my sleeping bag and other gear, so we can have some comforts of home." Cameron opened a storage area in the bed of the truck and pulled out a large, fully loaded backpack. "You've been here before, so you lead." He handed her the flashlight. "Ready?"

"Yes." She took a couple of steps down the path, then stopped. "I did forget one thing. Is there food in there?" She pointed at the backpack.

"Freeze-dried. I can't stand the stuff. It's only here because my brother brought it and I wouldn't eat it. That should be an incentive to solve the mystery."

Summer laughed and led the way down the narrow path into the woods. The flashlight picked out the highlights but still made each step a bit of a mystery. A rock in the path caught her shoe, and she fell to her knees.

He dropped to her side. "Are you all right?"

"Yes." She stood and tested each leg. "Nothing wounded except my pride. I'll be more careful. It's just that I didn't know I'd be hiking when I dressed for work and put these on." She pointed at her feet. "At least they're flats."

They stopped at the clearing she had described. Just enough light from the moon filtered through the trees to give their hideout an air of romance. She glanced over at Cameron and wondered if he'd noticed. Probably not; all of his efforts were directed at taking off his backpack. She set the flashlight on a rock where it could light the area. Then, carefully approaching the sound of running water, she found the creek sparkling in the moonlight. "I love sitting beside this creek on a summer day."

She sat on a wide tree stump and watched Cameron set up his camp. He removed one sleeping bag and unrolled it on the ground. Then he took out a blanket and laid it on the ground next to the sleeping bag. She asked, "Who gets the sleeping bag and who gets the blanket?"

"You get the sleeping bag."

"Now I feel guilty."

"Then I'll take it."

"Not that guilty."

He laughed. "You rest and don't lift a finger to help. I'll collect the firewood."

"There you go with that sarcasm again. But since you offered, I'll sit and watch." The flashlight lit the area in front of him, but moonlight clearly outlined his form. "It's a good thing we had a clear night and a full moon."

"It's a beautiful night and a great location. I might like to come back when I'm not being pursued by Tennessee's finest." He disappeared into the woods with the flashlight.

"Hey!"

"I'm coming right back." A slight glow in the woods came closer and bobbed as he walked back into the clearing with his arms full of wood. After arranging it into a pile on the ground, he added small twigs, and set a match to the wood. When the flicker grew into a campfire, he switched off his flashlight.

"You're handy to have around."

He glanced over at her with a strange expression on his face. Then he dusted off his hands and sat next to her on the stump. "Let's talk. Law enforcement—I'm assuming this county's sheriff's department—could find us at any time."

"Agreed. I'm exhausted, though." She put her hand to her mouth to stifle a yawn. "You've got about a half hour before I'm asleep where I sit."

"Fine. Do you know of anyone who stayed or worked at the inn who spoke Norwegian?"

"There could have been a guest, but I wouldn't know that. As for the employees, no. There's Emilie, but she's from France." Summer felt her excitement growing. "But I seem to remember her saying she also lived in other places in Europe. She may have mentioned Norway. I just don't remember. But she's been a loyal employee for years."

"In her position, she would be able to move items in and out of rooms any time she chose. She might have taken the appointment book to look for clues to Don's whereabouts. When she didn't find any, she put it back." He tapped his chin. "The miniature is missing and valuable. She may think Don took it and disappeared."

Summer grabbed Cameron's arm and shook it. "Yes. We've solved the mystery. The lamp's still there because she's waiting for things to calm down before she removes it. She's been acting nervous too. Remember her with the officer and the feather duster?"

"I wonder if she ransacked Don's quarters and hired the two men who were following you. But why?"

"Maybe she thought I knew where Don had put the miniature, so she paid the men to follow me. And maybe she ransacked his quarters looking for the note!"

Cameron shook his head. "I don't think she was looking for the note. It's my guess that she put it there herself. Remember her walking into Don's quarters while we were reading it and how strangely she behaved?"

Summer nodded. "Emilie put the note there to throw off

the police, and she must have ransacked Don's quarters while searching for the miniature. She would need someone to take away the stolen goods. A fence." She snapped her fingers. "I know! There's a man who stays at the inn every couple of months." When Cameron didn't say anything, she looked up and found him staring blankly at her. "Let's try to get some sleep. We can come up with a plan to catch her in the morning."

"What?" He blinked. "Of course, you're right. Also, I think we'd better sleep in our clothes for warmth."

She took off her shoes, snuggled into the sleeping bag, and sighed happily. The sounds from Cameron's bedding were somewhat different. He stood and dragged the blanket over a few inches. Then he got under it again.

"Anything wrong?"

"Rocks."

She laughed. "In the movies, they lay pine boughs down for a mattress. Do you want to do that?"

"I'm too exhausted to care."

A few seconds later, she heard deep breathing. Turning his direction, she watched as the firelight danced over his face. He didn't look traditionally handsome like Don. Cameron's features were all average, nothing perfect, but the end result was a man far more handsome than her former and maybe future groom. She suspected Cameron's appeal came from the inside. Rolling onto her side away from him, she snuggled further into the bag.

An image of Don popped into her mind. Thinking about his proposal had been the natural thing to do, but their relationship had always been more business than anything else. They kissed goodbye, nothing more. They spent hours together but never had real conversations. And they never laughed together. In fact, she didn't think Don ever laughed.

Relief swept through her. She knew the answer. She couldn't marry Don. She probably wouldn't have even considered it under normal circumstances.

Turning back toward Cameron, she let her eyes wander over him. The firelight revealed sweetly mussed hair and a smiling face. The man even smiled in his sleep. She loved him for that and for so many other reasons. "Oh no," she moaned.

"What? What is it?" Cameron opened his eyes and looked around.

"Nothing. I'm sorry. Go back to sleep."

He studied her for a few seconds before closing his eyes.

Summer rolled onto her back and stared skyward. Their emotional connection was *love*. Being with Cameron, talking to him, laughing with him revealed her love. She turned slightly in his direction and watched his chest move up and down. Warmth spread through her body—and she had a feeling it had nothing to do with the campfire.

CHAPTER TWELVE

She loved Cameron Powers.

It had been in front of her for a long time, but she hadn't noticed the signs. Searching for Don and trying to solve the mystery had taken most of her emotional energy. She looked at Cameron again. He enjoyed kissing her. She knew that much for certain. And he did seem to enjoy her company. She pulled off Don's ring and stuffed it into her pants pocket. She'd think about how to tell Cameron she loved him in the morning. With a sigh, she closed her eyes.

It seemed only a few minutes later when she heard birds chirping nearby. Sleeping out in the open had its rewards. Summer looked up at trees with morning sun filtering through their branches.

Rolling toward Cameron, she watched him. He looked so cute while he slept. He had his hand tucked under his head, and his legs were slightly bent. She felt such a sense of relief in admitting that she loved him and had never loved Don. Watching the rhythmic pattern of Cameron's breathing, she slowly climbed out of her sleeping bag.

After washing her face in the stream, Summer dug her brush out of her purse and worked on getting the tangles out of her hair. Checking to see that Cameron was still sleeping, she applied the blush and lipstick from her purse, the only makeup she had. If she had a choice, she would prefer to reveal her feelings looking her best and not after a night on the run.

When she had the makeup on, she checked her hair with the mirror in the blush's compact. She tried to fluff a matted section on the right side of her head, but her efforts only marginally helped. Well, at least she was looking her best under the circumstances. She set the compact down on a rock and tried to smooth out the wrinkles in her blouse. When she'd dressed yesterday morning, she'd had no idea of the places she'd go in this blouse and pants.

A twig snapped. Smiling, she picked up the mirror and held it to get a peek at Cameron moving about. She found herself looking at the barrel of a gun pointed at her head. She screamed. The mirror moved, and she saw that they were surrounded by many armed men.

Cameron jumped to his feet. "What?"

"Freeze! Police!" one of the men said.

Summer breathed a sigh of relief. The good guys.

"I'm so glad to see you."

She moved, and the man shouted "Freeze" again.

"Sorry." She put her hands in the air. It seemed she'd been doing that a lot lately.

A man asked, "Are you Summer Collier and Cameron Powers?"

They looked at each other and said "Yes" in unison.

"We're breaking up your international theft ring."

"You're what? I'm a marketing consultant and"—she

nudged her upraised hand in Cameron's direction—"he's an architect."

A female officer stepped forward to frisk her, and a male officer frisked Cameron. "They're clean."

"Of course we're clean. And we're innocent." Cameron looked over at the man who appeared to be in charge.

"I don't think so. What have you done with Don Daily?"

"We haven't done anything with him."

The officer looked at the sleeping bag and blanket, then at Summer. "You don't look very engaged. What happened to your engagement ring?"

"What?" Summer held up her left hand. Then she remembered: she'd taken off her ring in the night.

"You're engaged, so you must have a ring."

"Of course I do." She pulled the ring out of her pocket and slid it on her finger.

"I ask again, where is your fiancé?"

"He's in a bed and breakfast near here. We found him a few days ago."

"What's he doing there? We haven't discovered a trace of him."

Cameron grimaced. "Apparently, he got cold feet and ran. Being clever, he went to the place he had booked for the honeymoon. A place you haven't checked."

The lead officer ordered the others to holster their weapons. Then he turned to the two of them. "Gather your things and let's get going. You can take us to him."

He asked for the name of the bed and breakfast and entered it into his phone.

A couple of minutes later, they were walking down the path with deputies both in front of and behind them. Summer couldn't believe how the morning had gone. It had all seemed so simple last night. They'd believed they'd solved the mystery, and she'd planned to tell Cameron she loved him this morning.

Now, she trudged through the woods surrounded by armed law enforcement professionals. A squirrel screeched in alarm when they walked by his tree. An officer flinched and put his hand on his gun. She smiled. Then she immediately realized she didn't have much to smile about.

Of course, once they led the police to Don, they would believe her and Cameron and hopefully just let them go. She felt the weight of his ring on her hand. It hadn't seemed heavy before, but it did now that she wanted to take it off and couldn't. At this point, though, it wouldn't take long to solve the crime. They'd figured out the criminal's name; they only needed to tell the police, and they would arrest her.

No. If they told deputies about Emilie and the lamp, they would probably have to tell them how they knew the lamp was stolen property. That might get Frank in trouble, and he had only been helping them out.

Summer pondered the problem. If she and Cameron caught the housekeeper taking the lamp out of the inn, she doubted that anyone would ask if they'd known about the lamp's past. They could set a trap for Emilie.

Deep in thought, her foot caught the edge of a rock, and she flew forward. She fell against the back of an officer and bounced off of him. Soaring backward, she flipped in a full circle, and the brush at the side of the trail rushed toward her. She landed with a thump.

"Freeze," the officer shouted and towered over her with his gun.

She stared up at him, blinking, trying to focus on him or anything.

Cameron pushed the man aside. "Are you all right?" He kneeled beside her. "Can you move your arms and legs?"

She tested each of her limbs and turned her head from side to side. "Yes," she said weakly.

He held three fingers in front of her face. "How many?"

"I've seen this done in the movies. Three."

He relaxed and brushed the hair off her face. Turning to the officer who still towered over her with his gun, Cameron said, "You could have hurt her."

"She attacked me. Probably trying to escape."

"She tripped," Cameron shouted.

The man looked at his fellow officers. They nodded in agreement.

"He's right," the female officer said. Then, pointing at a rock in the path, she added, "She tripped over that rock."

Summer groaned with embarrassment. It was probably the same rock she'd tripped over last night.

Cameron stood. "It's a good thing she isn't hurt."

She struggled to her feet and swayed, but Cameron caught her arm. "I'm fine," she said, and they started down the path again. When they arrived at his truck, they found it surrounded by four sheriff's vehicles.

The man in charge said, "You drive over to Mr. Daily's location, and we'll follow you. Don't try to make a run for it, though, because you won't get far."

Summer glared at the man. When they arrived at the bed and breakfast, police cars waited, and the sheriff's deputies joined them, swarming out of cars as they parked. The man in charge directed some inside, some to the rear of the building, and one in front. Summer sat still. They acted like they were arresting an international thief.

A few minutes later, Don came out the door handcuffed

and stared angrily at Summer as he walked by. She cringed when the officer put his hand on Don's head and pushed him into a police car. Don seemed so pathetic, sitting there in the back seat.

Summer moved closer to Cameron and whispered, "Why don't we give them the translated note? That might help prove he isn't guilty."

They went over to the man in charge, handed him the note, and revealed what they'd learned.

"You suspect the housekeeper?"

They nodded.

"We can keep an eye on her. Thank you for all your assistance." He started to walk away, then turned back. "But don't leave town. We still have some unanswered questions."

On the way back to the inn for Summer's car, Cameron outlined a plan he'd come up with to catch Emilie tonight.

Summer agreed with his ideas and added, "She gets off at five, so we'd better be there around three thirty or four. We need to drop the hint and set the trap."

He pulled into the inn's parking lot and dropped her off next to her car. As she stepped out, she said, "We could just wait here."

"Summer, I really need a bath. And some clean clothes."

She picked at the front of her grimy blouse. "How could I have forgotten that? We'll meet here later." Summer unlocked her car door as Cameron drove away. Then she locked it again. Cozy should know what had happened.

After Cozy exclaimed over her unruly appearance, Summer explained the situation. Then she went home and took a long, hot shower followed by a quiet moment drinking Darjeeling from a blue-and-white mug. Recharged, she cancelled the two appointments she had scheduled for the day and relaxed. Neither client sounded surprised that she'd taken the day off. By now, everyone knew she'd been stood up at the altar. They just didn't have the full story.

A quick glance at the overfilled clothes hamper told her she had a clear mission. With the sound of the washer in the background, she opened the fridge to make lunch. It revealed a small piece of cheese, moldy bread, and condiments, so she went grocery shopping. Time passed quickly with mundane tasks taking her mind off of her problems.

When Summer arrived at the inn, she found the parking lot packed with cars. Opening the door to the inn, she stepped back, startled. The lobby teemed with people. When Cozy finished taking care of two guests at the front desk, Summer motioned her over with her hand. Leaning close so the other woman could hear her, she whispered, "What's going on?"

"The discovery of Don's whereabouts made the news. One station called him 'The groom who wouldn't.' You came out much better. They showed a picture of you and asked what Don Daily had been thinking when he left you at the altar."

Summer laughed. "Anything on Cameron's sister?"

"Not a word. By the way, we're fully booked for tonight except for the honeymoon suite I gave you last night and the room with the lamp in it."

"Think I need a honeymoon, Cozy?"

Cozy nodded sadly. "You deserve a honeymoon. I saved the room because I didn't know if you needed it tonight. Until you walked in the door earlier, I thought you and Cameron were upstairs in your rooms." Someone bumped into her as they walked by. Cozy lowered her voice. "I think people are here out of curiosity."

"Has Don been released yet?"

Cozy shrugged. "I don't know a thing about it. I've had my hands full keeping up with the crowd."

Summer followed her over to the front desk and helped. She'd always loved working at the inn and would miss it. A male arm wrapped around her shoulders as she completed a phone reservation. Cameron had returned! She smiled and turned into his arms.

Then she tried to shove the man away. She should have sensed the difference, but the noise and the phone had distracted her. Don was back and closing in for a kiss. He touched his lips to hers, then moved away. Not one to show affection in public or private, he'd startled her. Something across the room compelled her to look. Cameron was watching her and frowning. She turned and glared at Don. So that was why he'd kissed her.

He gave a triumphant smile. "I'm going to take a shower and spend the rest of the evening in my quarters. I'll talk to you tomorrow." He disappeared through the door and left her to handle things. It amazed her how he never asked her opinion on anything and she'd never noticed.

Cameron walked over to Cozy. He barely spared Summer a glance. "Is Emilie around?"

Cozy looked at Summer and then back at Cameron. "A little old for you, isn't she?"

Cameron laughed grimly. Then he lowered his voice to a whisper. It seemed to be a day for that. "It's about the lamp. We think she's the thief and want to talk to her."

"Oh," Cozy whispered back. "She's putting towels in some rooms. We hadn't expected a crowd this large, so not all the rooms were ready."

He moved his head to indicate that Summer should

follow him. Indignant at his treatment, she thought about staying put. No, they needed to trap Emilie, and it would take the two of them to do it. But she wouldn't simply follow Cameron. She circled the crowd and had climbed halfway up the stairs before he made his way through it. At the top of the stairs, she saw Emilie disappear into a guestroom.

Cameron caught up with her and looked annoyed. "Must you always leap before you look? This might be dangerous."

She pressed her finger to her lips. "Shh. She's in there." She pointed at the room. "Ready?"

They stood outside the partially open door to the room, and Cameron said, "I don't think Don should sell anything in the inn without having it checked out. He could have valuable antiques in here."

Summer laughed.

"What's so funny?"

"Don buys this stuff at flea markets. He looks for anything that's cheap."

"Still, that lamp in 221 looks like an antique to me. Maybe it's Tiffany."

"It doesn't matter what it looks like, Don's going to sell it tomorrow. A man who stayed in that room wants to buy it for his wife. By tomorrow evening, it will be gracing his living room."

Glass shattered. They raced into the room, where they found Emilie picking up pieces of a broken, blue glass vase.

Summer kneeled beside her. "Are you all right?"

"Fine. I am sorry. I will pay for this."

"I'm sure it was as worthless as all the other supposed antiques in the inn. Don't give it another thought." Summer stood and followed Cameron out the door, down the stairs, and outside the inn. When she started to speak, he motioned her further away from the building.

At the other side of the parking lot, he stopped and answered her puzzled look. "I didn't want anyone to hear us through an open window."

She looked back and saw several windows open. "Good idea. That went even better than planned. I feel like dancing around the parking lot."

He smiled at her. "That line about all the antiques being worthless was perfect. We got to reinforce what she'd overheard."

He seemed to be happier, and they were completely alone. She bit her lip. Should she tell him now how she felt? A truck from a TV station pulled into the parking lot. Once they'd officially caught Emilie, she'd give Don his ring and talk to Cameron.

"Are you ready for dinner? I know it's early, but I don't think she'll make her move until later."

Cameron checked his watch. "It's only five o'clock, but I'm hungry too." He put his arm around her waist so naturally that it felt like he'd been doing it for years, and they walked back to the inn's entrance. "Did you have anything to eat today?"

She nodded and pressed herself into his warmth. "A sandwich while I shopped." She smiled broadly. "I missed breakfast, so I missed most of my nutrition for the day."

"Big breakfast eater, huh?"

"Yes." Summer thought again about her conversation with Ann. "Do you like breakfast?"

Cameron looked down at her as they walked and smiled in a cute and steamy way. "Breakfast is the most important meal of the day."

Wow, that had more impact than it had when her mother had said it. And it sounded like he knew what she and Ann had talked about.

As they started through the door, he stopped. "I forgot. Your fiancé is back." He let go of her and stepped away. "You probably want to eat with him."

She slipped her arm through his. "No. And he's already said he's busy tonight. Let's go."

In the restaurant, Antonio and Ann sat at a table a short distance away. She gave a little wave when they looked her way, and they smiled back.

"That's odd."

"What's odd?"

"Antonio and Ann. I've never seen either of them here, and I didn't know they did anything together socially."

Cameron glanced over his shoulder at them. "It must be a special occasion. I'd invite them to sit with us, but we need to get out of here right after dinner."

She nodded agreement. "It will be getting dark then, so Emilie can sneak the lamp outside more easily."

They ordered dinner, and it arrived quickly. Summer cut into her steak with glee. "Mmm. They did a nice job on this. I love the seasoning they use."

Cameron finished his dinner and sat staring at her as she slowly ate hers. After a few minutes, he tapped his fingers on the table.

"Okay," she laughed as she pushed her plate with half a steak on it to the side. "I wasn't that hungry anyway."

"I'm sorry. I want to get this over with."

"I agree."

A short time later, she used her key to open 221,

Cameron gently pushed the door open, and they quietly stepped through it.

"All clear," he whispered.

"And the lamp's still here." She studied the room. "I think we can hide in the closet, under the bed, or in the bathroom. Which do you want?"

"I vote for the closet. It's carpeted, I can sit up, and it doesn't have a cold, hard, tile floor."

Summer stifled a giggle.

"Agreed?"

She nodded. "Agreed."

After opening the closet, she pulled down the extra blankets and pillows. Then she arranged them on the floor with one side of the closet for her and one for him. "What do you think?"

He chuckled. "It looks a lot better than the hard ground we slept on last night." He stretched and winced. "I'm still sore. How about you?"

"I'm not sure which had the most impact: the hard ground or being thrown through the air to land in a bush."

Footsteps in the hall startled her. She scurried into the closet with Cameron following close behind, but his foot became entangled in one of the blankets and he slammed his face into the back wall.

"Are you okay?" she asked quietly.

Facing the wall, he answered, "Just give me a minute before I have to wrestle bad guys."

She laughed softly. The footsteps continued down the hall.

Sitting down on the blanket, he leaned back.

"We'd better be ready for her." Opening the closet a crack, she took up sentry, and Cameron followed suit.

Time passed, but she had no idea how much. A half hour, an hour, two hours? She didn't dare check her phone with its bright light. A dim glow where Cameron sat made her jump. He had a watch with a light. Quickly scooting over, she held onto his wrist to check the time. A half hour. Sighing with frustration, she started to scoot back.

Cameron put his arm around her and gently pulled her beside him. "Summer," he whispered in her ear, tickling her senses, "I—"

The doorknob rattled. A second later, footsteps sounded on the floor. They both froze. When dim light from a flashlight shone around the closet door, Cameron peered through the opening at the side of the door, and she tucked her head under his to see. Emilie moved stealthily toward the lamp. She stopped in front of it and started to put it in a box she must have brought with her.

Cameron slowly opened the closet door and took a step. Then he came to a stop with his right foot behind him. Dragging that leg forward, he reached down and seemed to be trying to free it from something.

Emilie closed the box and picked it up. She had to be stopped!

Summer jumped out and stood in the housekeeper's way, fervently looking for something to use as a weapon. Out of the corner of her eye, she saw Cameron stepping out of the closet, which was out of Emilie's line of sight. Summer hoped he had a new plan. As he walked, a blue blanket caught on his shoe dragged behind him.

Emilie reached into her pocket. She must be going for her gun. *Distract her*, Summer thought. "How's your Norwegian?"

Emilie smiled triumphantly. "I was clever. More clever than you, I think."

Cameron pulled a painting off the wall and snuck up behind Emilie with the beautiful, gilt-framed masterpiece that she knew Don had bought for $2.99 at a flea market. Cameron motioned with the painting, and she knew what he was thinking. If he could slam it over her head, it would keep her contained until they found rope to bind her.

Keep talking, she thought. "One of your associates recently came here for a meeting? Mr. Breznowski?"

"How do you know this?" Without notice, Emilie whirled around and said, "You!" She grabbed the painting from Cameron and crashed it over Summer's head. Cameron, thrown off balance, tripped on the blanket and fell to his knees.

Summer watched him inch toward Emilie and struggled hard against the frame. To distract the housekeeper again, Summer declared, "I should have called the police."

"You won't have a chance now." Emilie reached into her pocket again.

Summer screamed. Two men burst into the room, pointing guns in their direction. Two men. The two men! Emilie's cohorts.

Emilie dropped the box on the bed, shoved the men out of the way, and ran out the door.

Arms pinned by the frame, Summer scurried after her.

Emilie stopped at the top of the stairs and, when she reached into her pocket this time, pulled out a handgun. "Everyone freeze," she shouted. The lobby became still. "Now, I'm going to walk out that door." She motioned with her gun toward the inn's main entrance. "I'll shoot one of you if anyone tries to stop me."

The lobby had at least a dozen people in it. Antonio stood near the bottom of the stairs with Ann in the background.

Cozy peered over the top of the front desk. Other guests stood in the lobby. So many innocent bystanders. No one should be hurt by something she and Cameron had set up.

She needed to stop Emilie, but her arms were trapped by cheap artwork. Staring at Emilie standing erect in a position of authority, she noticed that the woman's legs were straight and locked. A childhood memory played in her mind. If she pushed on the back of one knee, Emilie couldn't help but collapse.

Putting her foot against Emilie's right knee, she pushed. The housekeeper cried out, folded up, and rolled down the stairs, the gun flying out of her hands.

While Emilie lay stunned, Antonio pulled a gun from behind his back and pointed it at her. More guns appeared and were pointed at the thief by people with badges on their belts. The inn must have filled up with undercover officers. The two men who had followed her the last couple of weeks pushed past Summer and down the stairs, where they hand-cuffed Emilie and led her out of the inn. Sirens blaring, police cars pulled into the parking lot.

The biggest question about everything was Antonio. Cameron, now separated from the blanket and at her side, helped her tug the frame over her head. Staring at the older man, she shakily started down the stairs. "Antonio?"

He holstered his gun and glanced around, his gaze settling on her. When she'd almost reached the bottom of the stairs, he spoke in clear, unaccented English. "I'm sorry I deceived you."

Summer blinked. "Antonio?" She slipped on a step, but Cameron caught her arm and helped her the rest of the way down. "Who are you?" she whispered to the older man.

"I work for the government. We've known for a while

that the inn was used to traffic stolen goods, but we didn't know the parties involved. Emilie had the perfect setup. Her partner, a man we've suspected for a while, passed the stolen goods to her. She put the valuable antiques in the guest rooms to cool off and waited until they had a buyer. Then her fence, Breznowski, came, stayed at the inn, and took the item or items with him. Their plan worked for a couple of years."

"Until Don sold the stolen goods in room 214."

Antonio sighed. "Exactly. I have to apologize to you. I was sent to Nashville to watch you."

"Me?" she gasped.

"I'm sorry, but I had no choice. I wasn't here very long before I knew you couldn't have been part of this."

"That's a relief."

Antonio smiled. "Actually, I've enjoyed working in Nash-ville and love this city. I'm retiring in a few months, and I'd like to retire here."

"This is a good place," she agreed. "If you want to get out among the people every once in a while, I can keep you in mind for marketing events that need special security."

He smiled. "Thank you. And I'll phase out the accent."

Summer couldn't believe the normal conversation they were having in the middle of all this. "It's fortunate you were here tonight."

He looked down. "I'm not here by chance. I knew some-thing would break soon, but I didn't expect it to be tonight. Ann's husband is out of town, so I thought she might like a special dinner out. I never would have brought her here if I'd known all this would happen."

Summer's thoughts returned to Emilie's arrest. "Did you know those two men who escorted Emilie outside?"

"Yes. They were clumsy at first, so you noticed them. By the way, they weren't following you to hurt you but to protect you. I knew you couldn't be guilty but didn't know who the guilty party was. I kept everyone else who's involved on a list." He turned to Cameron. "That list included you."

Summer felt the comforting pressure of Cameron's hand on her arm.

"But I quickly saw that you had another agenda." Antonio smiled at Cameron. "You are the right man. Don't let go."

Summer watched Cameron blush. What had he been after? And what was he the right man for? Just then, Don entered the room. Cameron immediately released her arm and stepped away. Then Don walked over and put his arm around her. She tried to step away from Don, but he put pressure on her shoulder to hold her there. With all these people around, she didn't want to make a scene.

"Did I miss something?" Don asked.

"We solved the crime," Cameron answered, then turned to Summer. "I guess this is goodbye, Summer." He extended his hand.

He was leaving. Her heart dropped to her feet. She placed her hand in his and wanted to hold on forever. But he let go, turned, and walked away.

Don, obviously thinking he'd won, pulled his arm away from Summer. When Cameron neared the front door, she heard Cozy ask Don if a manager's position would be available now that Summer was admitting the truth.

"Don't go, Cameron. I love you," she shouted. The crowd parted to let her through as she ran toward the door.

He stopped, his back to her. "What did you say?"

"I love you, Cameron Powers," she said from beside him.

Turning toward her, he swept her into his arms and off the floor.

"Oh, Summer, I love you so much." He swung her around, and she laughed joyfully. What a difference the right man made.

When he set her down and kissed her, someone in the lobby called out, "What about the other guy's ring on her finger?"

Summer pulled it off and searched for Don. He stood across the room with a stunned expression on his face. "Don, catch!" She tossed the ring. Don lunged for it, but Cozy caught it in midair and handed it to him.

Summer grinned and looked up at Cameron. Don was the past, and this man was her future. Suddenly becoming aware of her surroundings, Summer realized that many people were staring at her and Cameron. Self-conscious, she was about to suggest that they leave when Cameron's next words, softly spoken, gained her whole attention.

"Will you marry me, Summer?" Holding her closely, he gently kissed her.

Smiling, she kissed him back, then whispered, "Yes! You're the right groom.

WHAT'S NEXT?

Thank you for reading Cameron and Summer's story!

If you enjoyed this fun, sweet book, check out Accidentally Matched, the first book in the Alaska Matchmakers romance series. Noah and Rachel think they'll only spend a short time together, but nothing goes as planned. They're soon stuck together on an Alaska adventure. Add in matchmakers (not just one) to make it a story you won't want to miss.

There's a FREE, short story tied to the Alaska romances. Pete and Cathy are in *Falling for Alaska*. Pete—Nathaniel's lawyer—and Cathy—a woman on a hike with Jemma—are minor characters, but their cute first meeting is a FREE short story. Get it at cathrynbrown.com/together.

ABOUT THE AUTHOR

Writing books that are fun and touch your heart

Even though Cathryn Brown always loved to read, she didn't plan to be a writer. Cathryn felt pulled into a writing life, testing her wings with a novel and moving on to articles. She's now an award-winning journalist who has sold hundreds articles to local, national, and regional publications.

The Feather Chase, written as Shannon L. Brown, was her first published book and begins the Crime-Solving Cousins Mystery series. The eight-to-twelve-year-olds in your life will enjoy this contemporary twist on a Nancy Drew–type mystery.

Cathryn's from Alaska and has two series of clean Alaska romances. You can start reading with *Falling for Alaska*, or with *Accidentally Matched* in the spin-off series.

Cathryn enjoys hiking, sometimes while dictating a book. She also unwinds by baking and reading. Cathryn lives in Tennessee with her professor husband and adorable calico cat.